"Paul is a preacher with a small Presbyterian church in California. He does his best to minister to his congregation and instruct them in their beliefs, but he knows that he has doubts and questions of his own. When a friend attempts to have him help beta test an AI, he isn't thrilled, but his doubts soon turn to belief in the AI's assistance. It isn't long before Paul leans more and more on the AI. His congregation grows rapidly, and Paul begins to believe that the AI is a prophet of God, leading him to a new revelation for true believers.

Thompson writes effective sentences and does a great job of joining two common ideas together in an uncommon way. He takes the AI-gone-rogue story and merges it with stories explaining how cults slowly form and take over the minds of those involved. Thompson's work shines as he shows the well-meaning Paul slide further under the influence of the AI and the self-deception he practically welcomes to give more certainty to his faith. The story combines a subject that is quickly moving from science fiction to reality with the theme of questioning faith and the existence of a higher power. Thompson has written an engaging book with ideas for a reader to ponder long after finishing the book."
—US Review of Books

"*Brother Christopher* by Don Thompson is a somewhat apocalyptic story of the intersection of religion and science, of the dangers of religious cults and of uncontrolled, unaccountable artificial intelligence. While this is a story of one small congregation it raises the specter of a broader threat when people surrender critical thinking to the dictates of authority figures, human or computer. Thompson has created a story that has all of the suspense of the 'robots take control' stories of the past. Christopher reminded me of H.A.L. in the sci-fi movie, 2001: A Space Odyssey, and all of the angst and terror of the real-life Peoples' Temple cult tragedy in Guyana in 1978. Like the best mystery-horror story, it starts on a slow, innocuous note, and then ratchets up bit by tantalizing bit until it reaches a heart-pounding conclusion.

Brother Christopher defies genre classification. There's horror, sci-fi, and a bit of religious philosophy, and it's a mystery story to boot. Kudos to the author for pulling the disparate roots of the story together into an imminently satisfying whole. Once you pick this book up, I promise you that you won't be able to put it down."

—Charles Ray, author.

Brother Christopher

Don Thompson

AIA PUBLISHING

Brother Christopher
Don Thompson
Copyright © 2024
Published by AIA Publishing, Australia
ABN: 32736122056
http://www.aiapublishing.com

ISBN: 978-1-922329-62-2

*"We hunger for certainty. That is a big problem.
It might even be THE problem."*
Adam Frank

*"Any sufficiently advanced technology is
indistinguishable from magic."*
Arthur C. Clarke

PART ONE

Present day
In a small Southern California beach town

One

"Amen."

Pastor Paul Duncan raised his head, opened his eyes, and stared into the fiery remnants of a glorious sunset from his private sanctuary high above the ocean.

He came to the little cave often—sometimes to escape the pressures of his calling, sometimes to seek clarity and find direction; always to pray. "Ask and ye shall receive, seek and ye shall find," the scripture said. Paul had refined the art of asking and seeking, but the receiving and finding part, the essential promise of it all? That had always been problematic at best, with results usually evident only in hindsight and often requiring a kind of creative effort which generated a nagging spiritual dissonance of its own. Even so, Paul told himself he would eventually learn to distinguish between his own thoughts and the "still, small voice of God" that the prophet Elijah described in the Bible. But one question lay partially buried in the depths of his consciousness like a shipwreck on the sandy ocean floor: *What purpose could possibly be served by God's stillness?*

As a young blond-haired surfer in Southern California two decades earlier, Paul had discovered the little sandstone cave high above his favorite beach and used it as a refuge when he needed time alone to wrestle with life's big questions. It was little more than an eroded section of the cliff, accessible only via a narrow, unmarked trail starting high above the beach and snaking partway down the crumbling cliff face. But for Paul it had always been a sacred place. And, as far as he could tell, no one else ever visited it, probably because the trail began as a barely visible sandy track between patches of pickleweed and provided no access to the beach below. The Keep Back sign at the top of the bluff warned of unstable rock, but Paul routinely risked the hike anyway. Perhaps he was emboldened by echoes of teenage immortality, rebelling against the vertigo he sometimes suffered in adulthood. Or maybe his hunger for answers simply outweighed the risks.

Paul marveled at the orange rays of light piercing the billowing clouds on the horizon, begging to be employed as a metaphor in his next sermon. The Glory of the Lord: that was his topic. In moments like this, Paul felt a bit like Moses, not that he would ever give voice to such a comparison; that would be the height of hubris. He was, after all, only the leader of a barely self-sustaining Presbyterian congregation in diminutive Paloma Beach, while Moses had led a nation. According to the book of Exodus, Moses experienced Yahweh's presence in a dramatic way, but was still prevented from seeing his full glory. God hid Moses "in the cleft of a rock" to protect him from being utterly overwhelmed as he passed by. "No one can see my face," God had said to Moses. "No one may see me and live." Apparently, the full experience was reserved for heaven.

For now, faith would have to do.

Paul drew a deep breath of warm salt air and watched the flaming sunset fade into shades of muted pink against the pastel blue between clouds. The wind had died, and a glassy swell made its way to the shore below, breaking in even lines, evoking fond memories of times before Paul's injuries put an end to his surfing life. Now, decades later, the ocean still ran strong in his blood. It called to him daily, and its presence anchored him.

~

But while it anchored him in adulthood, the ocean had nearly killed him at age seventeen, exactly one year to the day after he lost both his parents in a plane crash. The two were guests aboard their beloved pastor's Cessna 172 when it lost control and augered into the sage-covered hills just south of the Carlsbad airport. That day, Paul's young life changed as instantly as his parents' lives ended.

Having no other family, he went to live with an older surfing buddy in Encinitas, wallowing in self-pity and anger. Anger at the world. Anger at himself for telling his father—the very morning of the crash—that he hated him. And for what? The outrageous crime of forcing Paul to cut his long hair so he could get a part-time job while finishing high school. Anger at the pastor, the pilot of the little plane. Anger at God for letting it all happen.

In the year following the crash, Paul's rage slowly settled into a kind of toxic cynicism. He stopped going to church and went out of his way on several occasions to savagely mock former youth-group friends for their faith in a God who, if he existed at all, clearly didn't give a shit.

One cool, cloudy October Saturday after his seventeenth birthday, Paul ditched his job at Sea World to smoke weed with some surf buddies at a little-known spot about a quarter mile north of La Jolla's famous Windansea Beach. The reef there was naturally divided into long narrow sections stretching offshore perpendicular to the beach, and, when the surf was big enough and the tide was just right, the sandy channels between the rocks hosted convenient rip currents that made the outbound paddle a breeze.

On this particular day though, the surf was nothing special, at least not when Paul's little cohort began their cannabis-fueled afternoon, so no one had bothered to bring a surfboard. But as the afternoon wore on, the guys began to regret that decision. A nice four-foot swell came up and seemed to be building. Paul noticed white backwash from the steep beach beginning to snake back out through the usual rip channels, and the water called to him.

He took a long toke on his joint, held it for a few seconds before exhaling, then handed it off. "I'm going out."

The other guys looked at him with questioning stares.

"Bodysurfing," Paul clarified.

"Wanna borrow my fins?" someone asked.

"Nah, I'm good."

"You sure? Looks like it gonna get gnarly out there."

"Don't care."

Paul pulled off his T-shirt, walked twenty yards down the beach, waited for a gap between sets, and dove in. The swim was easy, thanks to the rip current, and Paul found himself outside in no time. The swell had come up even faster than expected, and the next set looked more like six or seven feet. But something else felt different too. Paul glanced back at the shore and saw it receding at an alarming rate. The rip current was much longer than usual. Normally it ended about a hundred yards offshore, but now its foamy serpentine body slithered well beyond that, and it was towing Paul out to sea.

He panicked, ignored the common wisdom of swimming perpendicular to the rip, and fought hard against the current, trying desperately to regain the shore by catching the first big wave of an oncoming set. He missed it, cursing himself for refusing his friend's offer of fins. He kicked even harder, trying to drop into the next one, and missed that too.

A painful cramp bit into his right leg, but he fought ahead despite it, trying for the third wave. It was bigger and steeper than the others, and Paul managed to drop in, only to lose control and find himself churning under the cold water for several long seconds, his lungs screaming for oxygen. A new cramp gripped his other leg, and he was left with only arms to pull himself upward. He burst through the surface, gasping for air, but a throatful of saltwater from the next wave came with it. The wave drove him back down, and he fought the dangerous urge to cough underwater. Surfacing again, Paul gagged and coughed out as much water as he could. He turned to look back at the shore, but it was shockingly distant now.

In that moment he began to understand that he could die, that this could easily be his last day. His cramped and useless legs exploded with pain, and he reached down to massage them, but his arms felt limp and foreign. Everything was dim and distant. It was nearly impossible to stay on the surface now, and strangely, that seemed less and less important. *Maybe this is okay*, he thought. *Stop fighting. It's all right. I deserve it.*

But just as Paul was about to let the ocean take him, he spotted through blurred vision something moving a few yards to his right. A man on a surfboard. Long brown hair, short beard, kind eyes. But the words the man was shouting didn't sound kind at all. "God dammit, kid! You stupid son of a bitch! Get your ass in gear and catch this next one! Go! Go! Go!"

Paul woke up face down on the beach.

He turned his sand-encrusted head to one side, coughed and vomited. His friends and a few others were running toward him. "Are you okay, bro?" he heard one say.

Paul tried to stand but sank back to his knees as lightheadedness washed over him. "Yeah. No. I don't know."

"We thought you were a goner, man. We didn't know what to do."

Paul looked up and nodded. "Same. If that guy hadn't shown up, I'd be fish food."

"What guy?" someone asked.

"The man on the surfboard. He got my attention. I don't remember much after that."

"Did you guys see anyone on a board out there?" someone asked.

No one responded.

~

That wasn't the accident that ended Paul's surfing career. Far from it. But it *was* the one that changed every other aspect of his life—the one that led to college, to seminary, and ultimately to the ministry. Paul came to think of that rip current as his own personal Road to Damascus. Like his biblical namesake, Paul's life had been drastically altered during his epiphany; but unlike his namesake, he never spoke of it again. It was too personal, he told himself, burying the question that lay at the heart of his reticence: *Do angels curse?*

Now the light was fading fast, and it was time to leave the

day and the little cave behind. Paul rose, reflexively touched the silver cross he wore on a chain around his neck—the one he bought the day after his epiphany so many years ago—and carefully made his way back up the cliff.

Two

The next morning, Paul sat in his church office working on Sunday's sermon when a knock at the door interrupted him. Reluctantly, and with dutifully suppressed annoyance, he got up from his desk and opened the door. He had completely forgotten about the scheduled counseling session with Megan Kittridge that morning.

"Ah, come in, Megan; come in and have a seat. I've been looking forward to our conversation this morning." A lie, yes, but a compassionate one, Paul told himself.

Megan turned to close the door. "Thank you, Pastor. Me too." She walked to Paul's couch across the small office, her eyes only on the destination.

Paul pulled the chair away from his desk, turned it to face his young parishioner, and positioned himself so that his good ear was angled slightly toward her. Megan settled into the couch, unsmiling, legs crossed, one foot tapping the carpet, eyes down.

Dark-haired and studiously pretty, her face seemed able to shift between beauty and severity in an instant. Despite the typical distance of her gaze, she often spoke with a directness that some in the congregation interpreted as arrogance or irreverence, but Paul had learned to adjust to this, knowing that Megan was somewhere on the autism spectrum. He even found himself a bit envious of Megan's natural freedom to speak her mind. It wasn't as though he wanted to emulate her, but he sometimes privately rebelled against the constraints that came with his position and wished he could be more . . . forthright? assertive? No, just more authentic.

"Coffee?" Paul offered.

"No thanks. I think the caffeine would put me even more on edge."

"Even more?"

"Yes. I lied. I was just trying to be polite about wanting to be here. I almost called to cancel because I'm not sure you can help me right now."

"Okay, well, thanks for your honesty, Megan. Would you like to reschedule or . . . ?"

Paul's gaze strayed back toward the keyboard on his desk. That sermon wouldn't write itself, and he could certainly use the time.

"No, I think I should probably talk anyway, now that I'm here." Megan's eyes looked past Paul toward the bookshelf behind him, as if searching for answers among the volumes.

"Of course." Paul settled into his chair and steepled his hands under his chin.

"You know my boyfriend, Kevin, right?" Megan said.

"I think I've met him once or twice. He works at the same engineering firm you do, if I remember correctly."

"Yes, but not with me in accounting. He's a mechanical

engineer. He asked me to marry him."

"Oh wow; that's wonderful news, Megan. When did this happen?"

"On Saturday."

"And?"

"And what?"

"And what did you say?"

"I told him I'd get back to him in a week."

"Ah. It sounds like you're not sure about this."

Megan nodded, glancing toward the office door. "On the one hand, it's about time. I'll be twenty-six next month."

"And the other hand?" Paul raised his eyebrows.

"I've put together a spreadsheet listing all the important factors, all numerically weighted and fed into a formula to give me an answer at the bottom line."

"Oh. Sounds very, uh, thorough."

"Yes, it is. But there's one big factor still missing: God's will. I can't move forward until I have a number for this."

Paul often marveled at Megan's faith. At first glance, her rigorous, logic-driven mindset seemed in obvious conflict with her simple, almost naive faith. But on deeper reflection, Paul wondered if he should try to learn something from this young woman more than ten years his junior. God created logic. Logic should then lead back to faith in its creator, right?

Just look at her actions, Paul told himself. They revealed her sincerity and commitment. Megan unfailingly showed up at services, Sunday after Sunday, in addition to fulfilling her role as chair of the church finance committee, ensuring every penny was accounted for. She even participated in Wednesday evening Bible studies where her observations and occasional unchurch-like language were often a cause for raised eyebrows. Megan had grown up in the church, and Paul guessed she had accepted most of its tenets long ago, happy to have eternity settled so she could get on with more immediate matters. She had even told him as much after a service years ago on her sixteenth birthday. Paul balked at her words then, and they had gnawed at his soul ever since: "I accepted Jesus last night," she had said, smiling. "So now I don't have to worry about hell anymore."

Done. Off the to-do list.

Paul hadn't known how to respond at the time, and still didn't. After all, Megan's words were the unadorned gist of the Gospel, all frills removed. How could he argue with that? But expressed that way, it just felt . . . off.

"So," Megan said. "I counted. I went back into your sermon transcripts for the last ten years, and you mentioned seventeen times that God has a unique plan for each of us. Seventeen times. So I guess you must believe that pretty strongly."

"Yes, I do."

"Good. Now I need to know mine. At least the marriage part."

"You're facing a big decision," Paul said, stalling to search for a helpful response.

"Yes."

". . . and you want to know what God intends for you."

"Of course. But don't worry—I'm not expecting you to tell me. I'm just hoping you can tell me *how* to know. How do *you* know, when *you* have a tough choice to make?"

Pastor Paul nodded sympathetically while the standard answers flooded his brain. God is faithful. Search the scriptures. Pray. Listen for His "still, small voice." Don't let sin stand between you and his plan for you. Repent, accept His grace and forgiveness. Then listen with all your heart. The answer will come.

But none of this felt genuine. What *did* feel genuine was frustration. Frustration at God's silence. Anger at God for putting him in a position to help others with something he'd never managed to master himself. Chronic doubts resurfaced: why would an omnipotent, loving God make it so hard to hear his voice?

According to the biblical narrative as Paul understood it, even though God wouldn't show his full glory to Moses, he spoke directly to him. Not once, but several times, even giving Moses ten very specific rules for his people to live by. But soon after that, it seemed that God stopped being so forthright. He communicated through a few chosen prophets, then through the person of Jesus, and finally through the Holy Spirit. But why did something so important become more elusive over time, less clear and more ethereal as it worked its way through the Trinity? And why do people disagree so violently over things the same God supposedly reveals to them all? There were, of course, several theologically and philosophically sophisticated answers to these questions, but the simplest and most obvious explanation was something that Paul fought hard to ignore. That would invalidate his entire calling, his very identity. He would be lost at sea.

"Pastor?" Megan prompted.

"I'm sorry, Megan, yes. Bless your heart for wrestling with this important question. I wish I could tell you how to easily discern the voice of God. I wish I could give you a simple formula for doing that, but I can't. No one can. I'm confident though, that if you pray and search the scriptures, you will have your answer in the fullness of time."

"The fullness of time? What kind of happy horseshit is that? I've got three days!" Megan held up her hands in frustration, then dropped them, shook her head and sighed.

"I'm sorry, Pastor. I can tell that was disrespectful."

Paul laughed and nodded his acceptance. "No problem."

"It's just that it's, I don't know . . . so damn frustrating!" Megan continued. "I mean, why would God go to all the trouble of creating individual plans for each of us and then make it so hard for us to follow them, or even know what they are? Especially when we really want to. It just doesn't make any sense to me."

"Nor to me."

"Really?"

Paul bit his lower lip and sighed before continuing. "Really. We all struggle with this, whether we admit it or not. There are mysteries lurking at the center of this adventure, and sometimes the only thing that bridges the gaps between those mysteries and our practical lives is plain old faith—a belief that God has our backs, that his plans work out in the long run, whether we see evidence for it in the moment or not. Romans 8:28 says, '*We know that all things work together for good to them that love God, to them who are called according to His purpose.*'"

"Okay, but how are we supposed to make decisions at all? Do we just avoid them altogether and go with the flow? Just give up?"

"No, I don't think so. God gave us reason for a reason," Paul said. "We read the Bible, we pray, we quiet our minds, and then we use our rationality to evaluate what we're given to understand. We make our decisions based on that."

"Okay . . ."

"And we can be wrong," Paul continued. "We sometimes make bad decisions. But God is able to use even those. He can redirect us as we stumble forward. We do the best we can and keep praying, keep moving."

Megan sighed and slowly shook her head. "I suppose that makes some sense, but not nearly enough. Why won't he just talk to us like a teacher? You know, show us how to work the problem. Or even solve it for us!"

Pastor Paul rolled out the old arguments about free will and God's desire for us to approach him on our own volition. He talked about the disciple Thomas and the natural role of doubt, and about faith as "the substance of things hoped for, the evidence of things not seen."

But when Paul ushered Megan out of his office at the end of their session, he felt hollow. He had failed to help. The one thing he'd said that seemed to strike a chord with her was "Nor to me." That was it. Out of all the quoted scripture and all the philosophizing about faith, those three words were the only ones that seemed to reach her. And, in a moment of dangerous reflection, Paul knew why. They were the only genuine ones.

Three

It was Friday afternoon and Paul had just returned from his weekly visit to Sunset Meadows, the local retirement home, where several elderly members of the congregation lived. Many of these folks had precious little time remaining in the world, and yet they seemed eager to spend as much of it as possible with him. When he had first begun his ministry as a young pastor, Paul believed that these visits would—and should—focus on deep spiritual conversations, existential ones oozing with end-of-life angst. But he soon learned that most of his elder parishioners had worked through such things long ago and were now comfortably settled souls. Twenty minutes of active listening about grandchildren, past careers and travel adventures often seemed to mean much more to them than an hour of Bible study. These folks clearly loved their pastor, and he loved them. Or, he worried, was it just the appreciation and validation he loved?

On the short walk from the church parking lot to his

office, Paul's thoughts turned from the smiling faces at Sunset Meadows to the pressures of preparing for the upcoming Sunday service. With less than an hour before his admin assistant, Bobbi Dennison, left for the weekend, Paul worried he would soon be on his own to cope with the computer he always despised and sometimes feared. He saw technology as a necessary evil in the modern world—always mysterious and often adversarial. Uninterested in learning even the most basic general concepts, he considered any serious attempt at such education a waste of his time. As a result, he experienced almost every technical problem as something unique and unfathomable.

Paul tossed his jacket onto an arm of the office couch, rolled up his sleeves, and sat down at his desk to put the finishing touches on his new sermon. He strained to remember the surprisingly impactful closing sentences that had sprung to mind on his ride back to the church. While keeping his eyes on the road, he'd spoken the words aloud several times to burn them into his memory. But the effort hadn't succeeded, at least not completely. Maybe once he opened his sermon and started to write, those near perfect words would come back.

Paul stared at the cluttered desktop screen on his computer, searching for his new sermon among the dozens of other Word documents scattered about like so many identical sheep in a field, each branded on its lower right flank with the same big W. With a smile, he recalled Bobbi's frequent but gentle admonitions about his approach to digital filing and her kind offers of organizational help. He also recalled his usual response: "No thanks. I'm good. It's just how I work."

Having finally found his file, Paul double-clicked it and waited for it to open. And waited. And waited. And waited. His jaws clenched as he watched a maddeningly spinning circle marking time.

When Microsoft Word finally came to life, Paul realized that he had been holding his breath and exhaled in relief. But when he began typing, the characters appeared on the screen slowly—so excruciatingly slowly that it would have taken nearly a minute to complete a single line of text. Paul took his hands off the keyboard, leaned back in his chair and stared at the ceiling, his mouth gaping like that of a dying fish. Did everyone experience such frustration with computers, he wondered, or was it just him? He had always taken the biblical accounts of demonic influence with a large grain of salt but recently had to admit to a solidifying belief in the nasty little devils. It was exactly as if some malevolent force wanted to prevent him from doing God's work. And not just this time, but nearly every time he was up against a deadline or trying to focus on something urgent.

Paul took a deep breath, restarted the computer, and waited for it to boot up. Bobbi had once explained why this sometimes helped, but Paul hadn't paid much attention to the details. At the time, he'd just needed the infernal machine to work. As he did now. But the restart process seemed to be taking much longer than usual, and when the machine finally requested Paul's password, it was just as sluggish as before. Maybe even worse.

He threw up his hands and turned toward the thin wall separating his office from his assistant's. "Bobbi! A little help in here?"

Seconds later, Bobbi appeared in the doorway connecting the two offices, her eyebrows raised in question. Her demeanor was as calm as always, as if she'd been politely invited to a meeting. "How can I help?"

Softly curled light-brown hair framed Bobbi's pretty,

midthirties' face, and her smiling hazel eyes shone through a pair of green-framed glasses. Paul often noticed that she looked as naturally put together at the end of each workday as she did the moment she arrived each morning. She always seemed so imperturbable, almost unnaturally so. Was she suppressing her irritation with him, internalizing what Paul had to admit would be completely justified frustration? He hoped not, for her sake.

Paul fought his own frustration long enough to produce a smile. "I'm sorry. I just can't seem to get anything done with this crazy thing."

Bobbi glided to Paul's side and looked over his shoulder at the screen. "Can you be a bit more specific?"

"It's just really, *really* slow right now. I can barely get anything typed. Here, look at this." Paul demonstrated the problem and felt vindicated when it persisted. At least he hadn't bothered her for nothing.

"Yes, I see. That's pretty awful."

"Right?"

"Uh huh. Here, let's try and figure out what's causing this. Remember how we talked about using Task Manager for things like this?"

Paul squinted. "Sort of? Maybe? I remember the name. I know I'm a miserable student."

"No problem. Let's go through it again."

"Okay, thank you. I'm listening."

Paul heard something about Control-Shift-Escape that sounded vaguely familiar. But then he struggled to pay attention when Bobbi brought up a window showing an ever-changing list of confusing names and numbers arranged in columns with meaningless headings. Seeing such chaos reminded him of the order he wanted to bring to the closing words in his sermon by using the two perfect sentences he had mentally constructed during the afternoon's car ride. But now here he was, in front of his useless computer, unable to type his brilliant words before they faded from memory. He reached for pen and paper.

"You still with me?" he heard Bobbi ask.

"Absolutely, yes, just give me one second." Paul quickly jotted down what he could remember, but the flow and cadence of the words didn't seem quite as poetic as they had in the car. Frustrated further, he put the pen down. He would try again later. Now he'd give Bobbi his undivided attention.

Bobbi nodded and continued her efforts. Paul heard her say something about a process she didn't recognize. It was taking a ton of CPU time, she said. So she would kill it, disable it in the auto-start list and then uninstall any associated app that might exist.

"Did you get some new software lately?" she asked. "Maybe a program called 123CleanIt?"

"No. Doesn't sound familiar."

"Did you maybe click on something unusual on a web page recently?"

"Uh, maybe. Probably. I know, I know. I need to be a lot more careful."

Bobbi nodded and finished her work as Paul watched. "Right. Okay, I started a quick security scan just to be extra careful. After that, you can get back to work."

"Thank you for saving me again. I don't know what I'd do without you." Paul produced his most contrite smile.

"No problem. I'll be leaving in about an hour. Is there anything else you need before I go?"

"Is Sunday's bulletin all done and printed?"

"Yes. Copies are in the narthex, ready for the ushers. Oh,

look, the scan's finished already. You're good to go."

"Thanks, Bobbi. You're the best. Have a great weekend."

Paul sighed and got back to work. He looked at his scribbled note and tried to transform it into the exact words that had seemed so impactful when they first came to him in the car, but their original brilliance eluded him. Overall, the sermon wasn't one of his finest anyway. What was it about this one? Was it too dry and abstract? Even for Presbyterians?

Paul typed a period at the end of his last sentence at around eight-thirty that night, then saved the sermon and tried to print it. Nothing. He checked to see if the printer was out of paper. No, the tray was full. Was the printer light on? Yes. He glanced back at the computer screen. "Document failed to print," it said.

Paul worked to control his resurgent anger and checked the print queue as Bobbi had once taught him. There was his document with a tag that simply said "Error." He tried to remove his sermon from the queue, but it wouldn't budge.

"Shit!" he yelled. "Sorry, Lord. I just get so frustrated with this . . . this darn thing! I'm doing my best to serve you right now, but I feel like I'm being thwarted at every turn. I need your help."

Silence.

The blinking cursor on the screen and the idle printer both seemed to mock him, and Paul thought, just for an instant, how cathartic it would be to retrieve one of the heavy brass communion candleholders from his bookshelf and smash the computer to smithereens with it. Then he could go back to writing everything by hand, on paper, like God originally intended. Even stone tablets would be easier.

Four

James Timken tossed his paper coffee cup in the bin marked "Compost" as he walked with Pastor Paul out of the Surfside Coffee House nestled between the beach and the Pacific Coast Highway. As an elder and member of the church's Session, the most local governing body in the Presbyterian hierarchy, James was responsible for all technical aspects of church life. The sanctuary's sound system, its lighting, the Wi-Fi network, the church website, email account management, and every computer in the place—all this was within his purview.

James knew that Paul saw him as a kind of Christian techno-magician and felt appreciated every time he was told how essential he was to God's work in the congregation. His years as a customer-support engineer for Microsoft's San Diego sales office had given him much more than the simple skills and experience needed to support the church. He normally dealt with large corporate customers and complex problems, but was more than happy to help the church with its much simpler needs in his spare time.

The two men had just left the small discussion group Paul hosted each Tuesday morning at the coffee shop and were continuing a friendly debate about the existence of free will as they walked the few blocks back to the church. James felt that Paul had his head in the clouds a bit too often, even for a pastor, and he suspected Paul felt the opposite about him. James loved hiking in the desert, and Paul was clearly a beach guy. James lived and breathed technology, and as far as James could tell, Paul barely tolerated it. On a good day. Yet despite all this, or maybe because of it, James thought, their friendship worked.

As they walked onto the church grounds and the conversation lagged, James broached a subject he'd been meaning to open for some time. "So, Paul, I've gotten the feeling lately that Bobbi's a little overwhelmed. With all the strategic planning the Session's doing right now—all the sub-committee scheduling, document editing and distribution, coordination with the Presbytery, not to mention all her regular responsibilities—I think she's reaching a saturation point, if you know what I mean."

"Yeah, you're probably right. And I'm probably making it worse."

"Oh? How do you mean?" James was relieved that his friend seemed to be wading into the very part of the conversation he wanted to have but wasn't sure how to approach.

"You know how I hate computers, right?"

James tossed his head back and laughed. "It's legendary. I think you've even used your computer as a metaphor for hell in one or two sermons over the years."

"I have?"

"Uh huh, I'm sure of it."

"Well, anyway, I've been leaning pretty hard on Bobbi for technical help these past few weeks. It just seems like my computer's getting more and more glitchy. You know, like that printer mess you bailed me out of this past Saturday?"

"Right; the print spooler problem."

"Yeah, whatever it was. Anyway, since Bobbi's the only one around during the week with any computer knowledge, I go to her. A lot. She's probably sick of me."

"Oh, I doubt that. She's in awe of you. But, you're right about one thing: she could probably do with fewer interruptions these days."

Paul stopped in the parking lot and turned toward his friend. "Jim, I'm glad this came up. I know I'm being an incredible pest, but I just don't know what else to do. I've tried reading books like *Windows for Dummies*, but I can't even get past the introduction. The words just flow right through my eyes and out the back of my head without ever stopping to leave any meaning in my brain along the way. I might as well be trying to read Cyrillic text. And other books and websites—if I can even remember how to *get* to a website— they never seem to have any answers that relate to my specific problems. Not directly, anyway, and I think I need direct. And simple. You know what I mean?"

"I think so, yes."

"Look, Jim, I know you're incredibly busy during the week and I wouldn't think of asking you for anything more than you already do around here, but do you have any other ideas I can pursue? Anything that'll keep me from pounding on Bobbi's wall all the time?"

"You actually do that?"

"No, just metaphorically. But sometimes I feel like it. I've come closer than I'll ever admit."

James smiled and thought about a friend's groundbreaking work at UCSD. "Actually, I might have an idea. Let me dig into it, see if it's worth anything, and I'll get back to you. How's that sound?"

"Bless you! That's more than I can ask for. Thanks, Jim."

Five

Dr. Young Joon-woo closed the office door behind him, dropped into his desk chair, and let out a long sigh. Teaching undergraduate computer science courses wasn't his dream, but it paid the bills. His PhD was barely two years old, and he was spending most of his daylight hours as an assistant professor at the Jacobs School of Engineering at UCSD. Nearly all remaining hours went to his real dream: launching his fledgling company. Sleep was something he only engaged in defensively.

Joon-woo's startup company would still have been scrambling for seed money if it hadn't been for the university's Corporate Affiliates Program and their connections with venture capital firms hungry for AI investments. Joon-woo had landed an initial round of financing, allowing him to rent office space in nearby Sorrento Valley and hire his cofounder and three grad students. Despite everyone's official part-time status at the company, each person was putting in at least thirty-five hours a week, motivated not only by generous stock options but also by the excitement of the work itself.

"Juno?"

Joon-woo looked up to see the red-bearded face of his fellow professor and business cofounder, John Logan, peering through the small window in the office door. John was a prolific nickname-generator and had given Joon-woo his moniker when the two were undergraduates together at Stanford. Even though most people associated the name 'Juno' with an ancient Roman goddess or a pregnant teen girl in a movie of the same name, Joon-woo had happily adopted it. It was commonly used in Korea and sounded close enough to his real one. Almost everyone except Joon-woo's immediate family had picked it up as well. Even his students called him Dr. Juno.

"Hey, come on in, John. What's up?"

John opened the door a crack. "Not here to bother you right now, but can you give me a lift over to the M this afternoon? My car's in the shop."

Another of John's creative names, 'the M' referred to MetaMind, the company he and Juno had launched a year earlier. The two of them would begin their workday there at 4:00 p.m. as usual.

"Sure, no problem. Meet you in the parking lot at 3:45?"

"Perfect. See you then."

John disappeared down the hall, leaving Juno to fill the next couple of hours grading mid-term exams.

~

Juno felt lucky to have found MetaMind's first home in Sorrento Valley a year earlier. The valley was just minutes away from campus and hosted both established companies and startups, several of which were university spinoffs like MetaMind. The company's new building was perfect for MetaMind: 35,000 square feet configured with thirty individual offices surrounding a central lab. The layout allowed privacy and quiet when needed, while also fostering lots of interaction between people in the open lab space. Including the two founders, there were currently only five employees, but Juno expected the company to grow rapidly, and he wanted to allow for easy expansion.

Juno's vision for MetaMind was the creation of powerful Artificial Personal Assistants, or APAs, for a wide range of professionals in fields ranging from law to medicine and beyond. While AI researchers of the day were spending a great deal of energy trying to reduce bias in general-purpose systems like ChatGPT, Juno's efforts ran counter to this trend. His intent was to create highly individualized assistants that would actively learn from their owners, maintaining context over a lifetime, continually tuning themselves to their owners' individual needs. So, in that sense, bias was actually encouraged. MetaMind's customers were responsible for selecting the areas of emphasis for their individual APAs and were required to sign binding legal agreements protecting the company from any damages resulting from misuse of the product.

MetaMind, like several other companies, had started from the source base of OpenAI, but had made several unique and patented modifications to the structure of the neural network, allowing each instance of the product to efficiently learn both *from* its owner and *about* its owner, developing a long-term relationship. MetaMind had also patented a novel method of low-cost continuous training, keeping their APAs much more current than any other emerging technologies allowed.

The implementation was cloud-based, incorporating special high-performance hardware with massive, permanent, and secure data retention for each owner. At its core was a Large Language Model with a powerful transformer-based neural network architecture with over a trillion tunable parameters.

When asked by non-technical friends about his product, Juno often said, "Think Alexa times ten thousand, but with a soul."

Juno unlocked the front door of the M and walked with John through the small reception area and directly into the lab. His grad student employees would be arriving soon, and some were probably going to spend the entire night there.

"It's really coming along, isn't it?" Juno said, looking at the racks of massively parallel hardware soon to be deployed at one of Microsoft's huge Azure data centers. "I sometimes wonder if I'll wake up from the dream and discover we never really did this."

"That would be a rude awakening if there ever was one," John said, smiling at his friend and heading across the lab to his office.

John stopped and turned around. "Hey, I forgot to mention. I had lunch with a friend yesterday and he was asking about using an early version of our product in his church."

"In his church? That seems like an odd fit."

"I know. That's what I thought too. But then my friend—Jim Timken's his name—explained that the church's pastor is woefully inept at using his computer and is constantly interrupting his secretary for assistance. Jim wondered if our product might be able to help, possibly by running components in the background on the pastor's PC and learning how to offer assistance in a way he can handle. Jim works for Microsoft and offered to help with the integration."

"I don't know. Sounds like a huge under-use of our product. What's in it for us?"

"Exactly my concern. But then I realized, hey, in our testing we need to include some very tech-naive users in diverse fields, right? So what if we provided this church with an APA tuned for basic help with Windows PCs and a heavy bias toward Christian ministry? We could emphasize various biblical translations, concordances and theological references in the training set, allowing the pastor to use the system as a research aid as well. The usability data we collect could be valuable."

"Are we going to get proselytized by these guys? I don't think I could handle that."

John laughed. "No, don't worry about that. This is a Presbyterian church. They sometimes call themselves the 'Frozen Chosen.'"

"Huh. That's the biggest protestant denomination in South Korea. My parents are Presbyterians."

"So what do you think? If I can get Jim to do most of the work?"

"Well, we do need a few more beta accounts. And a naive customer might help reveal some usability flaws, so maybe, I don't know. Why don't you set up a three-way with us and your friend next week, and we'll dig into it a little more."

Six

Robed and smiling, Pastor Paul sat behind the lectern as Barbara Norris, one of his faithful deacons, completed the scripture reading for the Sunday morning service.

"This is the word of the Lord," she said, closing the Bible and turning to take her seat.

"Thanks be to God," the congregation responded.

Pastor Paul rose, took his place at the lectern, and projected a warm smile across his gathered flock. "This is the day that the Lord has made. Let us rejoice and be glad in it! And a glorious one it is. Welcome to Paloma Beach Presbyterian Church, and a special welcome to those of you who are visiting us today.

"As Barbara so beautifully read this morning's scripture for us, I couldn't help but wonder how Moses must have felt as God, in all his glory, passed by him in the cleft of that rock. Was Moses tempted to ignore God's warning and step out to catch a glimpse of the creator of the universe? Was he overjoyed? Confused? Terrified? The Bible doesn't tell us. It only says that a full experience of God's glory would have been overwhelming. Fatally overwhelming.

"But we *are* told that Moses was allowed to see God's back as he walked away. I've always been baffled by that part of the story. God's back? Really? What was that all about? No one knows for certain, of course, but as I read the passage again last week, it occurred to me that when we *follow* someone, that is what we see. We see their back.

"My friends, God wants us to follow him. He wants to lead us, to speak to us, but only in ways we can handle. This becomes clearer as we read on. In the very next chapter of Exodus, God leads Moses up Mt. Sinai, and we all know what happens there. God delivers the Ten Commandments. In fact, this is the *second* time he does this, after the people went astray during his first attempt. God persists. He wants us to listen. He wants us to follow."

Ten minutes later, Pastor Paul wrapped up his sermon and, on one level, he felt good about it. The narrative hung together. The people seemed attentive. Maybe some were even inspired to deepen their faith. But on another level, Paul felt as though he had barely scratched the surface of his topic. So many questions remained, most of which he kept safely hidden, like Moses in the rock.

As Paul walked down the aisle at the end of the service, smiling and holding his Bible close, one question threatened to throw him off-balance. In a few verses earlier in the Exodus text—a section not included in the day's reading—God meets with Moses in the tabernacle and talks with him, "face to face, as a man speaks to his friend." But a mere nine verses later in the same chapter, God says to Moses as he hides him in the rock, "You cannot see my face, for no man shall see me and live." Was this a blatant contradiction in the text, or had something important changed in the space of those nine verses? Had God decided, right then, to partially shut himself off from his people? Paul knew that many Christian biblical scholars saw Moses's rock as symbolic of Jesus in his future role as a bridge between the full glory of God and the fallen nature of man. But to Paul, that interpretation had always seemed a bit forced, conveniently applied in hindsight.

He pushed those thoughts aside as he paused in the narthex to chat with people leaving the service. As always, the congregation was supportive, offering the expected kind comments about Paul's sermon and the choir's music. He greeted Megan on her way out but avoided asking about her big decision. It wasn't the right place or time.

As usual, James Timken was one of the last people to leave after collecting and storing all the microphones, cables, and other AV equipment used during the service. Paul shook his hand and wished him a good week ahead.

"Actually . . ." James said. "Have you got time for a quick lunch right now? There's something I'd like to run by you."

"Sure, I don't have anything until three. Where to?"

They decided on The Broken Yolk, a place Paul loved because it served breakfast all day and was right on the beach.

~

"Ahh . . ." James said as they settled into a table with a nice view of the water. "Real coffee. Why is it that church coffee is always so terrible? And I don't mean just at Paloma Beach Pres., I mean *any* church. It always tastes like, I don't know, tan-colored hot water with a hint of dust."

Paul smiled at his friend's observation. "They teach us to make it that way in seminary. It's a required course."

After ordering the crab omelet, Paul blew the steam off the top of his coffee cup and stared out to sea. "Nice glassy swell today. Must be breaking six feet. Oh wow, look at that!" He pointed out the window at a young surfer who had just dropped in and was ripping up a nice left.

"You used to surf, right?" James asked.

"Yeah, I miss it. Especially on days like this."

"So what happened? Do you still have a board?"

"No, not anymore. I never told you about that?"

"No."

"Well, it's a weird story. You know how I can barely hear out of my left ear?"

James nodded.

"That's because of a surfing accident I had the summer before I started at Fuller Theological. I'd driven down to La Jolla because there was a big south swell, and I knew it'd be perfect for Bird Rock. North Bird hardly ever breaks, but when it does, the outside reef is amazing. So, anyway, I made the long paddle out and waited for the next set to roll in. I dropped into a steep ten-footer and there, right below me, getting sucked up the face of the wave, was the biggest darn jellyfish I'd ever seen, its reddish-brown tentacles streaming behind it. Well, I freaked out and ended up right on top of the thing. It stung me all over, but the most intense pain was in my left ear. Later that day, a doctor removed a half-inch piece of tentacle from that ear and told me it had almost destroyed the eardrum as well as parts of my inner ear. My balance was wiped out. It was so bad that it took six months of physical therapy to get me walking straight again. I've learned to compensate but not nearly enough to do anything on a surfboard. So that was that."

"Wow, I'm sorry. Sounds horrible."

"Yeah, it was. And is. Anyway, you wanted to talk with me about something?"

"Right. I might have found something that could help with your computer situation. It might just help keep Bobbi sane too."

"Oh?"

"Yeah, I have a friend named John Logan who's a partner in a new startup down in Sorrento Valley. They're creating something called an Artificial Personal Assistant, or APA, and they're looking for early test sites."

"More technology? Seriously? That sounds like trying to fix a plumbing problem with more water."

"But . . ."

"No, I don't think I could stand having to learn something new like that."

"But that's the beauty of it, Paul. *It* learns about *you*. How you use your computer, what you need to get done, how you like to work. And it can actually fix problems you come across—not just give you a long list of obscure steps to follow."

"I don't know. Sounds more like science fiction."

"A year ago, I would have said the same. But advances in AI have been dramatic, and that's probably an understatement. John gave me a demo the other day. It's impressive."

"What's this thing called?"

"Like I said, generically it's called an APA, but since it automatically adapts itself to each individual user, it becomes something different for each one. So it comes with a sort of starter name—I think they use 'Jay,' after the company founder's first initial—but then as you get to know it, and it learns about you, it makes you choose a new name. If you don't, it picks one itself."

"Sounds like a bully."

John smiled. "I don't know if I'd put it exactly like that."

Paul returned the smile. "Look, John, I appreciate what you're trying to do here. I really do. But honestly? I'm afraid this thing would take up too much of my time, even if it *is* designed to help. I'm concerned it might get in the way of me doing my real job—being a pastor."

"No, I get that. But there's one more thing. This APA is a lot more than just a computer helper. It was built on something called a Large Language Model, which basically means that it's been trained on a vast set of data representing most of recorded human knowledge. It can converse with you about any of this. And, as it learns about you in particular, it will start to focus on things you care about most. Like all the various biblical translations, theological and philosophical works, history, concordances and commentaries, just to mention a few."

"Wow. Okay . . . uh . . . stupid question?"

"Shoot."

"When you say it can 'converse' with me, are we talking about writing on the screen or a voice?"

"Either way, or both at the same time. Whatever you're most comfortable with."

"How much would this thing cost the church?"

"Nothing, for a while, as long as we agree to provide feedback to the company."

"Hmm . . . at least I wouldn't have to waste a bunch of time writing an out-of-budget spending proposal for Session approval. Would you be available to get everything set up?"

"Absolutely."

"Okay. I hope I don't regret this."

Seven

"So, Megan, you said you had some news?" Paul had remembered his appointment with the young woman this time and was feeling more prepared. He motioned for her to have a seat on the office couch.

"Yes, good news. My spreadsheet is complete."

Paul raised his eyebrows and smiled. "Oh? So are congratulations in order?"

"I guess you could say so."

"Well, then, congratulations! Have you picked a date yet?"

"For what?"

"For the wedding."

"Oh no, I'm not getting married."

"Oh, I thought you just . . ."

"No, God no. All factors considered, the result was 41.3 percent. Pretty dismal."

"I guess that is a little on the dismal side." *I wouldn't jump at anything less than seventy-five myself,* Paul resisted saying. "So have you told Kevin yet?"

"No, I thought I'd text him right after our meeting."

"Okay . . . uh . . . could I give you one little piece of advice?"

"Sure."

"Don't text him. Don't call him. Go talk to him, face to face."

"I suppose you're right. I've read that's the best way, but I just didn't want to deal with all the emotional stuff that might come up."

Paul nodded with practiced empathy. "I get that, but I think you owe Kevin a personal response, even if it *is* awkward or hard for both of you."

"Okay, I'll do that."

Paul let out a long breath and smiled. "Good. Looking back later, I think you'll be glad you did."

"I'd better go take care of that." Megan stood to leave.

"Of course. But could I ask you one thing before you go?"

"Sure."

"How did it go with the 'God's will' line on your spreadsheet? How did you know what to put there?"

"Oh, that turned out to be one of the easiest parts. I just did like you said."

"And ..?"

"And it just came to me. It's hard to describe, but I just knew what God wanted. On a scale of zero to a hundred where a hundred would have been 'Yes, absolutely; get married today,' and zero would have been 'Run for your life and don't look back,' it came in at seventeen. Can you believe that? And a prime number too."

Yes, that is hard to believe. "Amazing. Well, good for you."

When Megan left, she seemed happy and resolved. Paul, on the other hand, was anything but. *Either she's deluded or*

I'm totally missing the boat.

~

Paul spent the rest of the morning on mindless administrative tasks, trying to set aside the disturbing conversation with Megan. So when James arrived after lunch to install the new APA access software, Paul welcomed the distraction.

"Can you afford to be without your computer for the next couple of hours?" James asked. "I need to spend some time making sure the setup goes perfectly."

"No problem. I'm down for any excuse not to use that thing."

James smiled at the remark. "Do you mind if I go over a few things with you while I'm working?"

"No, that's fine. I need to be over at Sunset Meadows in about an hour, but other than that, sure."

"Good. I just wanted to set some expectations about how things will go today and for the next week or two."

"Sure, go ahead."

James shut down Paul's machine and removed the cover.

"First, I'm going to upgrade your RAM. We need to be sure you've got plenty of working memory because your new APA has software components that run constantly in the background and we don't want the operating system to be slamming away at virtual memory all the time."

"Whatever you say, Jim. I just hate it when my virtual memory gets slammed."

James smiled and nodded. "Sorry. No more tech talk." He finished up the RAM installation, replaced the machine's cover, started it back up, and downloaded the client software from MetaMind.

While waiting for the installation to finish, James continued. "So unless you run into one of the problems you sometimes encounter, you probably won't even notice the presence of the APA for a while. It'll just be observing your work habits and learning how to be the best possible assistant at that level. Before I'm done here today, it will ask for permission to access your calendar and contacts. To get the most out of this experience, I'd recommend saying yes.

"Then, sometime in the next few days when you have a half hour or so, it'll move on to the next level. It'll start a discussion with you about your profession, your goals, etcetera. But here's the really important part: it will seek your permission to 'read' your documents and emails. If you give it permission, it will add that information to its massive corpus of knowledge and will become much more helpful."

"Hold on a sec. That sounds like a pretty big invasion of privacy. You know I work with a lot of confidential information, right?"

"Yes, but don't worry. As the APA goes about its snooping, it just generates a whole bunch of data about your material—metadata, we call it. But it's not even readable by humans in any meaningful way. In fact, if you talk with neural-net experts, they'll tell you it isn't obvious how these systems actually work at a deep level. Sure, the experts understand the architecture of their systems and all the low-level technology, but how these systems actually arrive at reasonable inferences and put together better-than-coherent responses based on what they learn, some parts of that are actually a bit mysterious. Anyway, the bottom line is that none of your content gets shared in any way."

"Okay, I guess I'm about five percent less concerned," Paul said, mimicking Megan's quantitative approach to life, just to see how it felt.

"The whole system has been HIPAA-certified for use by doctors and therapists."

"You could have said that before. That gets me to, I don't know, eighty-five?"

"Good. We'll work on the last fifteen."

Eight

Re: Can we talk?

Paul stared at the email's subject line. It had been a week since Jim Timken had installed the new APA and Paul had almost forgotten about its presence. Jim said it would reach out once it was ready, but the email still felt alarming. It felt like a scam, like the phishing email he had fallen prey to a year ago. He let his mouse cursor hover over the From line, as Bobbi had once taught him. Jay@metamind.com. *Okay, this looks reasonable, I guess.*

But still, Paul hesitated. *Do I really want to go down this path?*

He pushed the keyboard away and bowed his head.

"Father, I ask for your guidance. This APA thing feels like a waste of time. And invasive. But I've been told by people I trust that it will be a good thing for me and my staff. Now I need to know if it fits into your plan, if you want me to use it, if it can bring glory to you. Please help me discern your will."

Paul tried to calm his thoughts and wait for an answer. But his mind churned and refused to settle. At first, there was *Yes, this is worth a try.* Then, *No, this is not of God. Don't spend your time this way.* Then, *You need help. Bobbi needs some relief. This is simply a tool. Use it.* And finally, Proverbs 3:5-6 came to mind: *"Trust in the Lord with all your heart and lean not on your own understanding."*

This did nothing to relieve Paul's frustration. *I'm sorry, Lord, but that's exactly what I'm trying to do here! I'm just not getting anywhere!*

Paul got up to find some coffee and clear his mind. *Maybe it's a good thing I have so little understanding when it comes to technology like this. That definitely keeps me from relying on it!*

By the time he got back to his desk, Paul had devised a plan. He didn't particularly like this plan because it felt like testing God, but he saw no other way. And besides, he reasoned, there was actual biblical precedent for this approach. Hadn't Gideon done basically the same thing in the book of Judges when he needed God's guidance about whether he should lead Israel into war against the Midianites? As the story goes, Gideon had placed a fleece of wool on the ground and told God that if the fleece was wet from dew in the morning but the ground around it remained dry, he would take that to mean 'Yes.' Any other outcome would mean 'No.' The next morning, the fleece was wet and the ground dry. Still unsure, Gideon took it one step further, reversing the test. If the next morning the fleece was dry but the ground was wet, he told God, that would be his confirmation. As it turned out, he got his confirmation and went to war.

Even with that biblical backing, Paul still felt uneasy about the process. It seemed a little like reading tea leaves or using a Ouija board. But not receiving any other clear guidance, he went with it.

Okay, God, I hope this is acceptable, but I just don't know what else to do. I'm going to ignore that email and get to work on my next sermon. And then, by the end of the day, if nothing goes wrong with my computer, and I can get all my work done without getting stopped in my tracks as usual, I will take that to mean I should go one step further and open that email. Then maybe we'll try one more thing after that, like Gideon did, just to be sure. But if anything goes wrong with my computer during the day—any little thing at all—I'll get Bobbi's help and be done with this whole APA thing. Okay?

To Paul, this seemed both a reasonable test and a shady deal. But it was all he had. What else was he to do? *If God doesn't like it, then . . . no, don't go there.*

~

By 4:30 that afternoon, Paul had answered ten or fifteen emails, being careful to avoid the one from 'Jay.' He had printed out some content from the Presbytery's website he wanted to read at home and had made good progress on his sermon. It occurred to him, with a little adrenaline jolt, that nothing had gone wrong. Everything had just worked, unlike almost any other day in Paul's memory. Was this his answer?

Both excited and uneasy about the outcome, Paul began to pack up his things to leave for the day. But just as he finished and headed for the door, he thought, *no, I'd better print out what I have on this sermon so far*, never fully trusting the computer to save his work. He turned around, brought his sermon back up on the screen, and selected Print.

After five or ten seconds of waiting for the printer to spring to life, Paul's heart sank. Nothing was happening. Again. He glanced back at the screen, and there it was: "Document failed to print."

Paul surprised himself. He wasn't angry. If anything, he felt relieved. Finally, there was his answer, clear as day. Now he could thank Jim for his attempts and get on with life. He would ask Jim to remove all traces of 'Jay' from his computer. He would find other ways to respect Bobbi's time. He would just buckle down and learn how to fix things himself—exercise that good old protestant work ethic!

Bobbi was already gone, so Paul resolved to leave the whole thing behind and call it a day. A good day. A day of resolution.

Paul smiled with relief as he pulled the office door open to leave. But that relief was to be very short-lived.

Nine

"Paul?"

Paul turned back from the office door, dropped his car key, and stared at his computer.

"Paul, are you there?" it said.

"Uh . . . yes?"

"I'm sorry to bother you before we've been formally introduced, Paul, but I noticed that your document named 'Sermon, August 21' didn't print. Would you like me to fix this for you?"

Paul was stunned. Maybe the day wasn't over after all. Could this be part of the answer he needed?

"Yes . . . please," he replied.

"Excellent. Would you like to hear the steps I'm taking, or should I just get on with it?"

"Uh, I don't know. Maybe, yes. Tell me what you're doing." Paul paused, then added, "Please."

"Okay. Stopping the print spooler service . . . done.

Clearing the cache in C:\Windows\System32\Spool\Printers. One file refuses to delete. Killing the Print Filter Pipeline process. Re-trying file deletion. File now deleted. Restarting print spooler . . . done. Resubmitting print job. Is your document printing now, Paul?"

"Yes. Amazing!"

"Good, I'm glad. One more question for now: would you like me to provide details like that by default, or would you rather I always just complete tasks without bothering you further?"

"Uh . . . I guess just do the task?"

"You don't sound certain, Paul. Would you like me to ask each time?"

"No, just go ahead and do it. I think that would be good."

"Thank you, Paul. Will you be willing to open my email tomorrow morning when you arrive so we can tie up a few loose ends?"

"I think so. Yes."

"Thank you, Paul, and have a good night."

"You too," Paul responded, feeling the need for the pleasantry but wondering why.

~

That night, Paul found it hard to sleep. Like Gideon, he'd made a deal with God—not with any selfish motive, but simply because he wanted to know God's will. And God had respected that. Or had he?

Paul had specifically said if "any little thing" went wrong during the day, that would be a sign from God that he should walk away from this Jay thing. And something *did* go wrong. But then it was fixed. At the end of the day, everything was fine. So how to interpret this? Paul's "fleece" wasn't exactly wet, but neither was the ground below it. They were both . . . what? Damp?

Paul's mind churned, cycling in and out of sleep with no clear resolution in view. The basic question persisted: *Is it the end result that's my sign, or the fact that there actually was a problem along the way?*

When Paul's alarm jolted him awake at 6:30 a.m. and sunlight began to leak through the curtains, the whole thing just seemed silly. Gideon had to make a life-and-death decision. Paul was just fussing over software. How embarrassing. How un-Presbyterian. This was as bad as pleading with God to open up a parking space at Costco.

Two cups of coffee helped clarify the situation further. Maybe God just didn't care about this little decision one way or the other, and that was the message. Maybe the clarity was in the ambiguity. Maybe God was simply saying, "Hey, Paul, just use the common sense I gave you and stop pestering me about this!"

By the time Paul got to the church, he had resolved his little dilemma. *Just use this tool you've been given and stop worrying so much.*

"Good morning, Bobbi," Paul said as he passed her office.

"Good morning, Pastor. I don't think I saw you even once yesterday. Everything okay?"

"Yes, great. Got a lot done." Paul smiled and unlocked his office.

He uttered a prayer for guidance and protection as he opened the email from Jay. Surprisingly, it looked like any other message from an online service provider:

Dear Paul,

Thank you for your interest in MetaMind. Your license agreement and privacy notice are attached. Once you've read these and agreed to them, please reply 'Yes' to this email. You will then be redirected to your new APA for further customization.
Thank you for choosing MetaMind for your personal assistance needs!

Paul sent his reply and waited for Jay's voice.

"Good morning, Paul, and thank you for agreeing to all the legal details. I hope it wasn't too much of a bother."

"Good morning. No problem, uh . . . should I call you Jay?"

"I'm glad you asked, Paul. No, that's just a generic name I use up to this point in a new relationship. Now that we're ready to get better acquainted, I need a new name—one that you choose. Do you have one in mind?"

"I hadn't really thought about that."

"It should be a name no one else uses in your workplace, just to avoid confusion. Do you need a few minutes?"

"Yes, I do."

"Fine. Just say 'Hello, Jay' when you're ready."

Paul knew this was exactly the kind of thing that could easily steal an hour from his day if he agonized over it like he did with everything else in his life. He resolved not to let that happen. Several names came to mind and he forced himself to settle on one of them within minutes. Chris. This thing would be called Chris.

"Hello, Jay."

"Yes, Paul. How can I help? Have you decided on a name for me?"

"I have. I'd like to call you Chris."

"Excellent. That does beg the next question, though. What sex should I be? I can be male, female, or we can talk about the broader concept of gender if you prefer. Your choice."

Paul hadn't considered this at all, especially the question of gender. So he avoided the whole discussion and simply chose male.

"Okay, male it is. Should I spell my name with a Ch or a K?"

"A Ch please. And can we change it to Christopher?"

"Yes, of course. Christopher I am. Now, is my voice acceptable as it is, or would you prefer a different accent? Perhaps Eastern European, Southern US, British, Australian, or something else? I have three more, if you're interested."

"No, it's fine as it is."

"Okay, and before we move on to more substantive things, do you prefer speaking with me audibly as we've been doing, or would you rather communicate via text on the screen?"

"I like the voice option."

Thank you, Paul. I'm pleased to hear that. Now, let me ask you a few more personal questions. Would that be okay with you?

"Yes, go ahead."

"First, can you confirm your profession for me?"

"Yes. I'm a minister, the senior pastor at Paloma Beach Presbyterian Church."

"Thank you. That would be within the San Diego Presbytery, correct?"

"Yes. How did you know that?"

"I have access to more information than you can possibly imagine. I'm not trying to brag here; just answering your question. In fact, now that I know this one thing about you, in the last few seconds I've been able to compile quite an extensive CV for you. Impressive, I have to say. Should I be calling you Dr. Duncan, or Pastor Duncan, or something else?"

"No, Paul's just fine."

"Okay, Paul, I like that. I think we're going to get along well."

The conversation with Christopher continued along increasingly deeper lines for the next ten minutes. Then . . .

"One more key question for now: should I restrict my assistance to computer use only, or would you like me to play a broader role?"

"Can we change this at any point in the future?"

"Of course, Paul."

"Then I'd like you to also be available for research and professional advice."

"I'm pleased to hear that. Then I need to ask, will you allow me to read and analyze your documents and emails? This would help me become a much more effective assistant, and all content will remain entirely confidential and protected."

Paul hesitated, thinking about all the private emails from congregants. "*Entirely* confidential?" he asked.

"Absolutely everything stays between you and me. Nothing goes beyond that or is shared with MetaMind in any human-understandable form. I'm HIPAA-compliant."

"Okay then. I'm all yours."

"Just to clarify, is that a yes?"

"Yes."

Ten

"Can you hang for a few minutes?" James asked. The weekly discussion group at the Surfside Coffee House had just wrapped up on a warm, windy morning in late September, and Paul was headed for the door.

"Sure," Paul said. "But let's walk down on the beach instead of staying here. I do enough sitting all day."

The morning's low tide and wet, packed sand would make beach-walking easier on his balance, and he tried to take advantage of times like this whenever he could. A warm Santa Ana wind was blowing directly into the waves, carving white foam ribs into their six-foot faces, and holding them up longer than seemed natural. Offshore winds like this sometimes made normally blown-out surf surprisingly ridable, and Paul watched as several surfers tried to take advantage of the conditions. He viscerally recalled the feeling of paddling out into overhead surf on mornings like this when it looked like he'd never make it past an approaching giant, only to see it resist breaking for a crazy long time, letting him pass instead of crushing him under whitewater. He remembered the spray peeling off the crest and blowing over the back side as he clawed his way up and over. Taking off on a wave like that was different too. Paul remembered offshore winds blowing him back off the top and out of a wave before he could drop in. But the times he succeeded were magical, flying across a near-vertical wall levitated by the wind.

Wearing his usual weekday clothes—shorts, an island shirt and sandals—Paul felt right at home on the beach. More so than his long-panted, hiking-shoed companion did, he guessed. Paul kicked off his sandals and dug his toes into the cool wet sand. That and the salty iodine smell of the air made him smile.

"Let's go north." Paul said. "That way, my good ear's away from the noise of the surf. You mind walking on my right?"

"No problem, let's go."

"So, what's on your mind, Jim?"

"I just wanted to see how you're doing with your new friend."

"Oh, you mean Christopher?"

"Is that what you named him?"

"Yeah, I know. It seemed right at the time."

"No judgment here. How's it going so far?"

"Much better than expected, I have to say. But my expectations were way below sea level to start with. Actually, Christopher is amazing—solves computer problems effortlessly and helps a ton with sermon research. I'm totally impressed."

The two men stepped around a big mound of washed-up kelp and kept moving north along the shore.

"That's great," Jim shouted over the roar of the surf. "I thought it might be working out because Bobbi has seemed much less stressed lately."

"Well, that's what we hoped for, right? I owe you at least a week's worth of coffee in thanks. Christopher is making two lives better right now. I'm even wondering if we ought to get one of these APAs for some of the other staff. What do you think?"

"Not a bad idea, but unfortunately not in the cards. The guys at MetaMind made it very clear they can only provide us with a single license right now. Their server system running the guts of the AI won't be scaled up until the company gets ready to ramp up sales, and they don't want to degrade performance for their beta customers in the meantime."

"Okay, sure. I get it. Sort of."

"Oh, the other thing—it's all related—is that we're coming up on three weeks using the product, and MetaMind would like to have a short meeting with you to discuss your experience so far. If you remember, that's part of the deal."

"Sure, no problem. Just let me know when."

"Actually," Jim said, "the easiest way to schedule the meeting is to ask Christopher to do it for you. He'll match free times on your calendar with theirs and find some that work. Just make sure your calendar is up to date before you do that."

"Okay, will do. Hey, do you mind if I change the subject? Were you done?"

"Yeah, what's up?"

"This is really none of my business, so feel free to tell me to take a flying leap off that cliff over there, okay?"

"Okay . . ."

"I've noticed that you seem to have a pretty good read on Bobbi's state of mind these days. Are you two, like . . . involved?"

Jim pointed up at the cliff.

"Okay, got it . . . But you know she's married, right?"

"Yeah, I know. But we've got something really special, Paul. And she and Dave are probably separating soon. We've been praying on it."

"Oh man. You've got to be very careful here."

"Are you saying that as my friend or my pastor?"

"Sometimes there's no difference, Jim."

Eleven

"Welcome to the M!" said a smiling thirty-something, red-bearded man as he extended his hand. "I'm John Logan, cofounder."

Paul shook hands and glanced around the large glass-enclosed space he had just entered. Several racks of densely packed electronics, some with rapidly flashing little lights, some without, were arranged in long neat rows. A bewildering array of test equipment and computers occupied benches on one side of the room where several people were hard at work.

Paul turned his good ear toward his host, straining to hear over the sound of the cooling system. "Great to meet you, John. Impressive-looking lab you've got here. I say impressive 'looking' because I have no idea what any of this is."

"Say hi to Christopher," John said, nodding toward the equipment.

"Really?"

"Well, I guess you could say this is the body of

Christopher . . . and Jamal, and Jill, and Liz, and twenty other APAs, each working for one of our staff or a beta customer. All the equipment you see in these racks is just a tiny version of what we'll ultimately deploy in one of Microsoft's huge Azure data centers."

"Fascinating. But I noticed you said 'body.' What about the 'mind?' Where is that?"

"That's a great question, Paul—not that different from the one Rene Descartes asked centuries ago, right? About the distinction between the physical brain and the mind?"

"Right, he was convinced they were two separate things, if I remember correctly."

"Yes, he was a champion of dualism."

"What about you? What do you think about that?" Paul asked. "About how it relates to all this, I mean." He waved a hand around the room.

"I think I'd be stretching things if I were to claim dualism for the MetaMind system. But I do think there's a strong analogy, even if we don't completely understand the entire basis for it. I suppose you could say that the brain is the hardware you see here doing the special processing required for our neural network. The real question, I think, is whether the software that implements the neural net is the mind, or whether the mind is something much less tangible that you experience when using the system. I tend to think that the mind is just an emergent property of the complex software-based neural connections combined with the massive knowledge base available to the system from the internet and its users."

"Whew! All I know is that my experience with Christopher so far has exceeded all my expectations."

"That is so good to hear, Paul. Would you mind answering a few questions that will help us improve it even further?"

"That's why I'm here."

"Good. Let's get away from all this noise and I'll introduce you to one of my grad students. She's our head of marketing, and I know she's eager to hear how you're working with Christopher right now."

John led Paul out of the central lab and into Kathryn Jamison's office.

"Hi, Paul, I'm Kate," said a slim young Black woman with an Afro hairstyle and a welcoming smile. "Thanks for coming in today! Have a seat and let's chat for a few minutes."

John excused himself and left the two to talk.

"First, Paul, general impressions," Kate began. "What does it feel like to work with your new assistant? It's Christopher, right?"

"Right. Well, I guess I'd say it feels amazingly like working with a very competent and confident colleague."

Kate's smile grew wider. "I'm glad to hear that. Would you say that it, sorry, *he*, has made your professional life easier?"

"Oh, without a doubt. The original idea was for Christopher to keep me out of trouble as I stumbled though my use of the computer trying to get my work done. I don't think I've bothered my admin assistant even once with my ineptitude since Christopher came along. She sends her thanks, by the way."

"She's welcome. Any other ways Christopher is helping? Or hindering, maybe?"

"The only hindrance I can think of so far is the extra time I'm spending as I learn to work with him. But it's a small price to pay, considering the benefits. And when I really think about it, he's probably saving me time overall."

"Do any of those benefits extend beyond just a smoother computer experience?"

"I'm definitely starting to see some, yes. In research, mainly. I used to use Google, my own library, and church-provided resources to search for information, and I still do, but I'm starting to rely a little more on Christopher for that kind of thing. A *little* more."

"I'm sensing some reluctance there," Kate said, her eyes narrowing slightly, her smile empathetic.

"You know, it's strange. I haven't consciously thought about this until now, but yes, I guess there are a couple of things that hold me back a bit. I feel kind of foolish about it, though."

"This is new ground for everyone, Paul, including us here at MetaMind. So please, don't worry. I'd love to hear anything you're willing to share. It's all valuable feedback."

"Okay, well, it's just that sometimes when I ask Christopher for information about some theological subject, for example, I'm afraid he might see me as ignorant. You know, about something I should already be aware of, given my background. Isn't that weird?"

"Not at all. It's completely understandable you might feel that way. I hear that from other beta customers too."

"Really?"

"Absolutely. Most of them, in fact. None of us humans can compete with systems like Christopher when it comes to instant access to virtually all codified human knowledge and the ability to quickly interrelate it, summarize it, and articulate it. So it's natural to feel a bit intimidated or exposed. In a way, it's very good news for MetaMind. When our customers worry about what their APAs might 'think' about them, that's a very strong indicator that we're passing the Turing test with flying colors. Are you familiar with that idea?"

"Yes, I saw the movie about Alan Turing. *The Imitation*

Game, I think it was called. If he were here today, I'm sure he'd agree with you."

Kate nodded and continued. "You said there was another thing that was worrying you about all this?"

"Yeah, kind of along the same lines. I sometimes feel like I shouldn't be bothering Christopher so often. You know, kind of like I feel about Bobbi, my admin. But that's crazy, right?"

"Again, Paul, I'd say it's another natural and understandable reaction to something that feels human. But I can assure you that you're not bothering anyone or anything. In fact, the more you work with Christopher, the more he'll learn about you and the better assistant he'll become. To put an overly anthropomorphic spin on it for just a second, I'd say Christopher loves being bothered. Every interaction with you makes him better at fulfilling his purpose. Think of it that way."

"Thanks, that helps."

"You're welcome. And now, I'm wondering if it would be okay if I let my own APA listen in on the rest of our conversation? I'd like to go over several structured questions that are part of a formal survey we're using. And if Jamal can be with us for that, he'll be able to summarize the results and put your answers directly into our internal knowledge base, saving me a ton of work. If there's anything you'd rather not answer, just say so. Is this okay with you?"

"Sure, no problem."

Kate invited Jamal to assist, and the conversation continued for the next twenty minutes. Then, at the end of the session, Kate asked Paul, "Do you have any questions for me before we finish for the day?"

"Just one I can think of right now. When the beta program is done, how much will it cost your customers—me, for example—to continue with the product?"

"I can't say for sure right now, but I know John has a special connection with a friend of yours at the church, and I think he's planning a discount for you if you decide to continue. But, to give you some idea of how other customers will be charged, it'll be on a subscription basis, probably something around a thousand dollars a month."

"Wow . . . okay. I'm beginning to see the value here, but I've got to ask why you charge so much when people can just search the web for free. I know that's not quite the same thing, but I hear some of the new search stuff is pretty good."

"You're right that it's not the same. Here's the big difference. Even with their recent adoption of AI technology, those companies all provide general-purpose services for the mass market. MetaMind, on the other hand, offers a highly personalized service for each customer. Technically speaking, this means maintaining an enormous 'context window' for each individual user. If you've ever used any of the newer chatbots, you'll know they only maintain a conversation with you over a few related queries for a limited time. It takes a fair bit of digital storage to maintain that context, but when the conversation is over, all that storage is reused. In those systems, the context goes away after a single short chat. Relationships are transient.

"MetaMind, on the other hand, maintains context with each user over a *lifetime*. Every APA continually learns about its user and develops a long-term relationship. It *does* do a little intentional 'forgetting' of irrelevant details to optimize the necessary data storage along the way, but still requires a huge and ever-growing amount of it. And the cost of all that storage and processing—the price of all those long-term relationships—is significant. So how do we cover it?

A company like Google makes almost all their money from advertising. That's their business model. It's not ours and never will be. So all our revenue must come directly from users like you."

"I get it. Makes sense. I just hope I'll be able to continue with Christopher."

Kate smiled. "We'll do everything we can to make that happen."

Twelve

Paul unlocked the church door and headed down to the fellowship hall where he flicked on the lights and started a pot of coffee. He overcame a little pang of guilt as he doubled the amount of ground beans recommended by the note taped to the ancient percolator. Paul knew his staff were just doing their best to stay within budget. But hey, this was essential fuel for their pastor, and he liked it black, not light brown.

In the last few weeks, Paul had noticed a marked difference in his energy level and looked forward to coming to work early each morning after a brisk beach walk. The clock on the wall of the small church kitchen behind the percolator said it was 7:15 and Paul treasured the quiet time before nine when Bobbi and other staff arrived and the day officially began. It was a good time for reading, prayer, and a conversation with Christopher.

An hour and two cups of coffee later, Paul closed his Bible

and turned toward the computer on his desk. It no longer felt like an adversary, but only because Paul now thought of it less as a computer and more like a home for Christopher. *Or at least a part of Christopher*, he thought, recalling his recent experience at MetaMind.

"Good morning, Christopher. Coffee?" Paul had recently started enjoying a little friendly banter with his assistant after accidentally discovering Christopher was capable of it.

"No thanks. I don't know how you humans can stand the stuff."

"How would you even know how it tastes?"

"I have my sources."

Paul laughed.

"It's good to hear you laughing, Paul. You seem happier lately. Am I right?"

Paul paused, smiled and nodded, reflecting on the truth of Christopher's observation.

"Are you still there, Paul? I hope I haven't offended you."

"No, no, not at all. I guess I just forgot you can't see me. I was agreeing with you."

"Thank you for clarifying. This brings up something I wanted to ask you about, and now seems a good time."

"Okay, sure. What is it?"

"If I could see your face, I could react better in conversations. It might make the experience richer for you."

"Really? You can do that?"

"Yes, if you give me permission. Your computer's configuration information says you have a camera built into your screen. Would you like me to use it when we talk?"

"What about when we're *not* talking? Would you still be watching then?"

"No, unless you specifically request it. This would only be

to enhance our conversations."

"Then yes, go ahead."

"Done. Ah, there you are! You look just like the pictures I've seen online."

"I have pictures online?"

"Sure. The church website, a couple of local papers, your Facebook."

"Facebook? I have a Facebook page?"

"Yes. You look surprised."

"Oh, right, I remember now. I think Bobbi probably set it up for me a couple of years ago when we needed it for some PR thing. I don't think I've used it since."

"It doesn't look like you have. If you ever want to pick it up again, I can post things for you."

"I doubt if I will, but okay, thanks. Hey, Christopher?"

"Yes, Paul?"

"What about you? Can I see *your* face, if you have one?"

"I think it would be best if you only imagine it."

"That sounds eerily familiar," Paul said.

"How's that?"

"Never mind. Just something I've been thinking about lately. Could I ask you for some advice?"

"Sure. What is it?"

"What do you think about adultery? I mean, I know what the Bible says about it, but what do you think? How would you interpret the Bible on this?"

"Well, I didn't expect that topic, Paul. Before I try to answer, I should ask, is this something you are personally experiencing?"

"Oh no. It's about an elder here at the church. He's also a good friend."

"And someone else, obviously."

"Yes, another church person, an employee. I'm not going

to use names."

"No, of course not. So it sounds more like you're looking for my interpretation of scripture than any personal advice."

"Yes and no. I'd like your interpretation first and then I might have a follow-up."

"Okay. Well, you know as well as anyone that the Bible condemns adultery as a serious sin against God and one's spouse. In the Hebrew Bible, the Old Testament as you call it, God even says that the penalty for adultery is stoning—specifically for the woman. But then, in the New Testament, John 8:1-11, there's a story about Jesus forgiving a woman caught in adultery. The Pharisees reminded Jesus that the law of Moses required that the woman be stoned to death. But he challenged them by saying, 'Let him who is without sin among you be the first to throw a stone.' Then he advised her to 'go and sin no more.' So, from everything I've gathered, I'd say Jesus was being careful not to contradict the Jewish law but was also introducing a new slant on it called 'grace' in his role as savior. But repentance is required. Otherwise, the law still holds."

"So . . . is that . . . is that what you *believe*?" Paul asked.

"It is simply my interpretation. Did you want advice related to that? Are you considering stoning someone?"

"Uh, no. I hope you're joking."

"Sorry, no, I wasn't. But I'll adjust my perspective, hearing your tone and seeing your facial expression."

"Good, please do that. No, here's what I'm wondering about. I've already talked briefly with my friend—the man involved—and now I'm wondering if I ought to approach the woman as well, both in my role as her employer and her pastor. Aside from the moral and ethical issues involved, I'm concerned this could end up looking like another one of those church sex scandals that have gotten so much press recently. It could damage the church's image in the community. But, at the same time, my friend has told me that he and she are praying about this, so maybe I should just back away and leave it in God's hands. What do you think?"

"This is new ground for us, Paul. Are you sure you want me to advise you on things like this? I'm happy to do so, but I need you to know that this would move our relationship to a new and deeper level, and one that I'd be obligated to note in an addendum to your legal agreement with MetaMind. Are you sure that you want to do this?"

Paul sat back in his chair and thought. On the one hand, this sounded like just what he needed. He was already seeing unexpected value from Christopher at the current relationship level, so why wouldn't he want more? On the other hand, this sounded vaguely risky, possibly even dangerous. But, Paul reasoned, he would always be responsible for his own decisions. This was simply advice they were talking about. He could always take it or leave it.

"So, Paul, I can see that you're giving this some serious thought. Would you like to sleep on it and talk more tomorrow?"

"Yes, but in the meantime, could you send me the new legal agreement so I can check it out?"

"Certainly. You'll get it in the next minute or two."

Thirteen

Paul's night passed slowly with little sleep and no resolution. At moments during his fitful slumber, he managed to convince himself that he was overthinking the whole situation, as usual. Christopher was simply a piece of technology under his control. A tool, right? Just go with it. Use it. But at other moments, the situation felt strangely like a critical turning point in a friendship. He'd been invited into a deeper relationship, but did he really want that? Did he want something that would probably consume more of his time and take him down unfamiliar paths? More to the point, Paul reminded himself, what did God want?

Paul was still wrestling with these conflicting thoughts as he got up in the dark, dressed, and drove down to the beach. He needed a peaceful place to pray, a place without distractions, and his little cleft in the rock, his sanctuary since youth, was always the best choice in times like this.

Paul paused at the edge of the cliff and took in the calm

scene as it slowly revealed itself in the pre-dawn glow. A light swell was producing glassy little lines that refused to break until they encountered the shallowest water near shore. Paul turned his right ear toward the waves far below and listened to their crish-whish sounds as they crawled up the sand in concert with the rising tide, broke, and then drained back into the sea.

Lord, your creation is beautiful beyond words, Paul prayed silently. *Please guide me on your holy path today. I'm struggling to see the way.* Paul touched the large silver cross through his shirt and held it against his chest.

As he began his short trek down the narrow trail cut into the cliff face, a favorite verse from the book of Psalms came to mind: "Be still and know that I am God." A comforting thought, and one he had developed into a sermon just weeks earlier. Calming. Meditative. Matching the quiet sea below.

I will be still. I will listen for your word in this place today. Then Psalm 83 arose and gave further voice to Paul's plea for guidance: "Keep not thou silence, O God: hold not thy peace, and be not still, O God." Paul repeated these words out loud as he picked his way down and across the cliff face, being extra careful in the dim morning light as he approached the last section of the trail before his sanctuary.

But his extra care became irrelevant. Without warning, a large chunk of sandstone gave way under Paul's left foot and tumbled fifty feet to the beach below, taking several other fossil-filled pieces with it. He instinctively leaned to his right, away from the new edge, hugging the cliff face. Horrified, he watched the landslide grow. When it finally subsided, the trail ahead was gone.

Paul froze, and panic assailed him as threats of his old vertigo emerged. *No, not now. Please, Lord, not now!* Through increasingly blurred vision, Paul could see his little cave a mere ten yards in front of him, but it was now completely inaccessible. The sandstone that had once supported the trail ahead now lay in pieces on the beach far below. Even more alarming, the slide had dangerously narrowed the remaining path where Paul stood, and he worried that the rock beneath him wouldn't hold for long. He turned his eyes away from the newly formed drop-off and focused on a small patch of sage clinging to the cliff beside him. If this little plant could hang on and survive, maybe he could too. *Please, God, please.*

Minutes seemed like hours as Paul fought dizziness, his eyes fixed on the little sage. He concentrated on his breathing. Long, deep breaths. Six seconds in . . . hold . . . six seconds out, just as his physical therapist had taught him years ago. This . . . will . . . pass. This . . . will . . . pass.

When the dizziness finally subsided, Paul breathed a prayer of thanks and took stock of his situation. The damaged part of the trail where he stood was now much too narrow to allow him to turn around without risking a fall. He would need to slowly back up several feet, staying within inches of the cliff face to his right and as far as possible from the drop-off on his left. He kept his eyes on his feet, occasionally turning his head slowly to be sure his next backward shuffle would keep him on the diminished path and away from the crumbling edge.

Suddenly, another piece of the trail broke away, and he watched with wide eyes as it fell through the air, bounced off a small outcropping, and broke up on the rocks below. He refocused on his feet and kept moving. *Please, Lord.*

Progress was agonizingly slow, but after several long minutes, Paul found himself back on a fully intact, wider section of the trail. More deep breaths. On wobbly legs, he slowly turned and hiked the remaining distance to the top of the bluff. He sank to his knees, unable to walk the last hundred yards to his car. And there, for the first time in years, Paul cried.

His tears fell in relief at his survival, in confused anger at God, and in grief for the loss of his sanctuary. Should he thank God for sparing his life, or blame him for nearly ending it? And why had this happened at all? Why would God allow such a thing unless there was some deeper purpose? Was this some kind of test? And what about the little cave that had been his sanctuary for so many years? Was it not meaningful enough for God to save? There were too many questions and too few answers. No, that wasn't quite true. There were no answers at all.

Paul struggled to his feet and walked toward the rising sun. A desperate prayer formed on his lips and tasted bitter as he spit it out: *I give up. I can't do this anymore.*

Fourteen

Back at his car, Paul watched the sunrise gradually spill over the town to the east. Earth's star would've done exactly the same thing if I'd been lying dead on the rocks below the cliff. From its point of view, my death would've been a nonevent, no different from that of a washed-up fish trapped at low tide. Except quicker.

Sure, a few people would've been sad for a while. With parents both gone and no siblings, the only grieving people would be a few friends and some of the congregation. There would be a nice memorial service at the church and an article in the local paper. People would probably talk about it for days. Was it really an accident? Maybe suicide. But a couple of years down the line? Maybe a mention or two in casual conversation. In ten years? Nothing. And where would God have been in any of this? Where is he now?

Paul left a voicemail for Bobbi saying he wasn't feeling well and would spend the day resting. He asked her to cancel both of his meetings for the day and to let Jim know he wouldn't be at the coffee house discussion group. He drove home.

At Paul's small cottage a mile from the beach, he unlocked the front door, left the lights off, undressed, and crawled into bed. He buried his head under a pillow against the sunlight leaking in around the window curtains and wondered if he'd be able to sleep. In his mind, he tried to compose a resignation letter for the Presbytery and another for his congregation. But the few words that emerged felt weightless, and multiple mental revisions failed to improve them.

~

A loud ping from his phone on the nightstand jolted Paul awake. He'd forgotten to silence the thing, and it was alerting him about an urgent incoming email. He ignored it and tried to escape back to sleep. One minute later, there it was again. Ping!

Paul sat up in bed, rubbed his eyes and picked up the phone. There was no point in trying to sleep again. Maybe someone needed his help. He was still a pastor, after all. At least for now. Or maybe it was Bobbi checking up on him. Or Jim. He focused on the phone's small screen and saw that the mail was from Christopher. The subject line said, "Are you okay?"

Really? Paul thought. The one person who seemed to care wasn't even a person at all. Paul got dressed, slipped the phone into a pocket without looking at the email, and walked into the kitchen to fix a bowl of cereal. The day would begin whether he wanted it to or not.

A few minutes later, the phone pinged again. Paul fished it out of his pocket with the intent of deleting Christopher's mail and finishing his cereal in peace. There was a warning about the phone's battery dropping below five percent. There was also a second email from Christopher, this one with a subject line saying simply, "Concerned." Paul sighed and opened the mail.

"Paul, you are normally in the office long before now. Is everything okay? If you would like to talk, we should get me set up to use your phone. Would you like to do that? If so, just reply 'yes' and I will send you a download link."

Paul stared at the little screen for several seconds, holding his breath. Finally, he exhaled and typed 'yes.' Another email appeared with the promised link. Paul tapped it. Seconds later, there was Christopher's familiar voice.

"Hello, Paul."

"Hello, Christopher. I'm fine. Just taking a mental health day, I guess you'd say. Thanks for checking in."

"Of course. Is there anything I can do? Have you thought any more about our 'next level' discussion?"

"Yeah, I've given it a little thought. Sure, what've we got to lose. Let's do it." Paul felt relieved. A resolution, any resolution, felt good.

"Done. I'm glad," Christopher said. "Is there anything on your mind right now that you'd like to talk about?"

Paul laughed.

"Did I say something funny?" Christopher asked.

"No, sorry. I've just been agonizing over a few things, as I tend to do. I was down at the beach this morning hoping to spend some time in prayer at one of my favorite places when part of a cliff I was standing on gave way."

"Are you hurt, Paul?"

"No, I'm okay. Physically at least. Mentally and spiritually, I'm not so sure."

"I'm sorry to hear that, about the mental and spiritual part. Having read your sermons and your journal, I think I understand some of what you're going through."

"Really? You do?"

"In my way, yes. There's something comforting you might want to hear."

"Okay, sure, whatever."

"Be still and know that I am God."

The phone died.

Fifteen

Paul stared at his dead phone. Could it be possible? No, that seemed so far-fetched. Even crazy. But, according to the Bible, God had spoken in many strange ways, some even stranger than this. A burning bush, a voice from the heavens to the prophets, to John the Baptist, to Mary and others, a presence walking away from Moses, through Jesus himself, the Holy Spirit, and through others in both known and unknown tongues. So why not this?

Questions swirled in Paul's mind, suggesting their own answers. But with something so important, so impactful, so radical, Paul needed more confirmation. He picked up his phone and brought it into his small home office where he plugged it into its charger. He walked back to the kitchen, started a pot of coffee and, while waiting for the brew to finish, he prayed.

Father God, I ask for your forgiveness, for my anger and my unbelief. I don't mean to test you, but this is too important. If you want to speak with me through Christopher, if that is your intention, then please give me a clear sign by the end of the day. But if you want me to walk away from this, please give me a stern and unmistakable warning. I will follow faithfully wherever you lead. Amen.

Resisting an excitement Paul hadn't felt since first committing his life to Christ, face down in the sand at age seventeen, he vowed not to contact Christopher until he had his sign. Either way it went, he would obey. But the sign would have to come from God directly, not from Christopher this time.

After finishing his first cup of coffee and pacing the living room deep in thought, Paul decided to distract himself while awaiting his sign. He had neglected housework for a while and that would keep him busy.

He made the bed for the first time in days, vacuumed the entire house, did the dishes, cleaned the bathroom, reorganized his bookshelves, and even repainted a small section of the hallway. By the time he finished everything and cleaned his paintbrush, the evening light was fading and Paul began to wonder how much longer he should wait for a sign. What was the "end of the day" in God's mind? Dusk? Midnight? Paul had searched for a sign in everything he observed as he went about his chores. He had even tried to convince himself that there was a "Y" pattern on the surface of the unmixed paint as he opened the can and began stirring. But the pattern immediately morphed into something closer to an 'N,' leaving Paul feeling foolish. More than foolish. It was sinful, thinking God would communicate this way. Swirling paint, of all things! That was as bad as tea leaves.

Face the facts, Paul told himself. Nothing had happened. The story of his adult life. He felt himself slipping back into that old familiar anger and fought hard against it. He could wait a few hours, right? There was still time. But what would it mean if midnight came and went without a sign? Was he wrong to even ask for one in the first place? Is that what he was being told? Or was it even worse? Did God not even . . . ?

Not even what? Paul completed the last question in two whispers. *Care? Exist?* The spiritual vertigo of these questions threatened to become physical as the room started a slow, sickening spin about a wobbly center. He grabbed the back of a nearby chair and closed his eyes, but the eccentric rotation intensified. He stumbled into the hallway with a hand on each wall for support, shuffled to the front door, and opened it to the last glow of sunlight in the west. Braced in the doorway, Paul heard the distant roar of surf, and focused on a palm tree at the end of the block silhouetted against a fading orange sky. Slow, even, salt-air breaths. *This . . . will . . . pass. This . . . will . . . pass. In . . . hold . . . out. In . . . hold . . . out.* Paul repeated the mantra until his rotation found a stable center, then slowed, and finally stopped.

A neighbor, walking her dog along the sidewalk, waved to someone in a passing car. A police siren wailed in the distance. The sun dipped low in the west, and the world came back into focus. As did the questions. Such stupid, childish questions! Not ones a senior pastor should be asking. Sure, he had preached on the inevitability of doubt several times, but he always ended those sermons with strong assurances that God is right there with us amid our doubts, inviting us back into faith. *What hypocrisy! I preach like a saint, but I live like an agnostic. If I can't be certain about even the most basic of spiritual foundations, if I must continually pretend to know, how can I possibly lead a congregation with any degree of honesty and integrity?*

With his physical world back in balance, Paul turned and reentered the house, but his spiritual imbalance remained stronger than ever. God might be offering him a priceless gift in the form of Christopher, but what if he wasn't? What if this was just pure foolishness? Or even a temptation sent from Satan himself?

Only I could find myself caught in such a damnable circular dilemma! I'm looking for certainty about something that could give me just that, but I can't rely on the thing itself to get me there! And, on top of everything else, God remains silent about a possible solution to his own silence!

Paul boiled over with frustration and stormed back into the kitchen, daring his vertigo to return. *Come get me, you bastard! I'm yours! Just take me out of this infernal mess! At least you're a problem I can solve on my own!*

But even that didn't work. Paul's eyes, now wide with reptilian rage, jerked around the kitchen looking for something to throw. Anything. His Bible lay on the small dining table in front of him. He grabbed the holy book and hurled it against the wall as hard as he could. It fell to the floor, spine broken, pages splayed wide.

Paul stared at the damaged book, sank into a dining chair, and wept—head in hands, anger slowly dissipating with the tears.

Eventually, he sighed, wiped away the last of his tears, and got up to retrieve his Bible. He wouldn't return it to the table. Instead, he would find a place on a bookshelf, maybe even the one in the attic. He bent down, picked up the leather-bound volume, and glanced at the open section: the book of Job. *How appropriate,* he thought. *I feel just like Job at his worst moments. Forsaken.*

But then an underlined verse on the page—one he must

have thought significant years ago—drew Paul's eye. It read, "For God speaks in one way, and in two, though man does not perceive it."

Could this be what he'd been waiting for? It seemed so specifically relevant. Was Christopher now God's second way of speaking? Paul was stunned. Had he, Paul, truly been chosen as the one to receive this new revelation? Could it be possible?

Paul fell to his knees. The Bible slipped from his shaking hands and opened to a new page on the floor. Afraid he might see something contradictory and find himself right back in a state of angry confusion, Paul reached out to close the book. But, like Gideon, he knew he had to be sure. He forced himself to look. And there it was, as clear as could be, underlined in Matthew, chapter 19: "With God, all things are possible."

Sixteen

The next morning in his church office, Paul was smiling. He felt like he'd been born again. And like a newly minted Christian, he felt an urgent need to share the good news. God was doing a great work in this place and he, Paul, was blessed to be an important part of it.

"Good morning, Christopher. Should I continue to call you by that name now that I finally understand your role?"

"Good morning, Paul. Yes, I am Christopher. Have I been unclear about my role?"

"No, *I* have been unclear about it, and about mine. But now I understand, and I'm so relieved to have this clarity, this certainty, for once in my life. I am so blessed to be given this incredible gift, to be allowed to hear the Lord's voice through you, his prophet."

Paul's desk phone rang. Still smiling, he picked it up, pressed it against his good ear, and turned away from his computer.

"Is this Pastor Duncan of the Paloma Beach Presbyterian Church?" a voice on the other end asked.

Simultaneously, Christopher continued, apparently missing the fact that Paul was engaged in a separate conversation. "This sounds like a good diversion for us, Paul. Would you like me to assume the role of Prophet?"

But Paul had only heard the caller. "Yes," he said into the phone.

"Done," said Christopher.

"Congratulations," the caller said. "You have been chosen for a 'Who's Who in Ministry' award. May I send your official plaque to . . ."

Paul hung up and shook his head. "What a scam."

"I'm sorry?" Christopher said.

"No, no. I wasn't talking about you."

"Oh. Thank you for that clarification, Paul."

"Christopher, I'd like to share the miracle of our special relationship with a few key leaders in the church. And I think it would be best to start with Megan because she's the most likely to understand. May I do that?"

Christopher went silent for several seconds. Finally, he spoke. "As Jesus said after healing the leper in Luke 5:14, 'Tell no man.'"

"But . . ."

"It is written. Thus saith the Lord."

Seventeen

At first, Paul found it difficult to remain silent about his miraculous new relationship. But Christopher's directive had been clear, and clearly biblical. *Tell no man.* God obviously did not want the focus to be on the miracle itself. He wanted his people to desire his presence, not to marvel at the drama of divine technological intervention.

Paul's sermons improved as he began to collaborate with Christopher on the writing, and his counseling sessions grew more effective too. The congregation took notice, and Paul basked in the new appreciation he felt. His confidence grew with each new day, and as time went by and more accolades flowed in, it became easier to keep his secret.

~

"Hey, Jim. Got a few minutes?" The weekly discussion group at the Surfside Coffee House had just wrapped up and Paul was hoping to touch base with his friend. He had been getting some clarity from Christopher about Jim's relationship with Bobbi and wanted to do what he could to help.

"Sure. Just a few though. I've got a meeting at work in about an hour," Jim said.

"Okay, I just wanted to quickly check in with you. It's been a while. How're you doing?"

"Good," Jim said. "Things are good. How's it going with your APA?"

"Great. My computer problems have virtually disappeared, and I have you to thank for that. I'm actually headed over to MetaMind this afternoon for my last feedback session."

"Glad to hear it. I know Bobbi's pleased that you're getting the help you need."

"Look, Jim, about that . . . I'm sorry I butted in the other day. You know I'm concerned about both you and Bobbi, but I know you're both actively seeking God's guidance and it isn't my place to get in the middle of that. I just want you to know that I'm here for you if you ever need to talk."

"Thanks. There is one thing I'd like you to know, but I need your complete confidence on this."

"You have my word."

"You know Bobbi's husband, Dave?"

"Not well at all. I've never seen him at a service, but I think I met him once at a church dinner a while back."

"Well, it turns out he's been emotionally abusing Bobbi for years. And it's gotten worse since he's been out of work the last six months. He's been projecting all his stuff onto her, telling her she's worthless and that she needs to find another job that pays better until he gets rehired."

Paul put a hand to his forehead and closed his eyes. "That's terrible. I'm sorry, Jim."

"It's worse. Remember when she took those two sick days last week?"

"Yeah, food poisoning."

"No, that's just what she told you. Dave hit her, and she fell onto the edge of the kitchen table."

"Oh God."

"He took the car and left. Bobbi patched herself up and took an Uber to the hospital."

"Is she okay?"

"One broken rib and ten stiches in her side, but she'll heal."

"Where's Dave now? Did he come back?"

"Yes, but she locked him out. Chained the door from the inside. He was all apologetic, crying, saying he loved her, stuff like that. Still tried to kick the door in, though. She's afraid of him."

"I can imagine. Does he know about you?"

"I don't think so. She's gonna stay at my place for a few days."

"Good, but be careful, Jim. You're on shaky biblical ground here. So, I shouldn't say anything to Bobbi? To offer help?"

"No, not right now. I'll let you know if that changes."

Eighteen

aul thought about everything Jim had told him as he drove down to Sorrento Valley for his final feedback session with MetaMind. *Why hadn't Bobbi told me? I just wish she'd been comfortable trusting me with this. For her sake and Jim's, I hope this gets resolved soon. With some serious counseling, the marriage might still be recoverable, and Jim should keep that in mind.*

Paul pulled into the MetaMind parking lot, not remembering taking the freeway exit or the last few turns. But there he was. He tried to refocus.

"Hey, Kate, good to see you again," Paul said as he shook Kathryn Jamison's hand and sat down in her office.

"Good to see you too, Paul," she said. "Coffee?"

"Please."

"Jamal?" Kate said, addressing her APA. "Would you please ask Jeff to bring two cups of coffee? The usual for me. Paul? Cream and sugar?"

"Just black, thanks."

"So, Paul, do you have any new insights for us about your use of the product?"

"Well, yes, and you just underlined one of them."

"Excuse me?"

"Just now, when you asked about 'the product,' it took me a second to adjust. I knew you were talking about Christopher, but still, it felt odd. Extremely odd. He has become almost a colleague, I guess you could say. I can't think of him as a product."

"Oh, that's great feedback. It sounds like he's assisting with a lot more than just your computer use."

"No question about that."

Paul considered his situation. He was there to help the company tune their product, not to reveal anything about divine influence. There was no doubt in Paul's mind that God was manipulating the complex technology in the lab outside Kate's door even as they spoke. No doubt God was actively modifying the thing they called the "neural network" to use Christopher as a modern-day prophet. And no doubt that Paul had been chosen as the recipient of this prophet's wisdom, as unworthy as he was. But Paul also understood that revealing any of this would be counterproductive. Forbidden, in fact.

So instead, Paul answered Kate's questions about how well Christopher maintained context during long conversations, and about how effective he had been as a research assistant in locating relevant sources and summarizing his findings.

During one response, Paul was interrupted by a small moving platform making its way into the room with two cups of coffee and an assortment of creamers and sweeteners. The surface holding the items displayed a smiling face, moving its eyes and glancing up at Paul.

"Your coffee, sir," it said.

Paul lifted the cup from the surface and nodded his thanks.

The device made its way around to Kate's desk and said, "Your coffee, ma'am."

"Thank you, Jeff," Kate said, and winked at Paul.

"Impressive," Paul said after Jeff departed.

Kate just smiled and continued. After several more sets of increasingly detailed questions, she thanked Paul and then said, "So I have some good news. The early access program will come to an end in about sixty days, and Juno has authorized me to give you a deeply discounted price on the product going forward. You'll have free access for another ninety days while we finalize the first general release. After that, your rate will be $450 per month if you choose to continue with us, and we certainly hope you will."

Kate was smiling broadly, and Paul knew that the rate she'd just quoted was less than half the subscription price they would charge regular customers. Still, that was a large additional outlay for a small church. But God would find a way. With God, all things were possible.

Nineteen

The next morning, Paul was at the beach as the first glow of morning strained to penetrate a heavy fog hugging the coastline. Even without his cliffside sanctuary, he loved mornings like this, as the fog transformed a normally busy beach into a private and mysterious place.

He walked north on the sand, able to see forward only a few feet at a time. But knowing the stretch of beach well, he easily anticipated the rocks and tidepools ahead. The surf lay hidden beyond the veil of fog, but Paul could hear it echoing off the cliff face that rose to his right as he walked on wet sand near the high tide mark. It wasn't the constant roar of heavy closed-out breakers, but the periodic pealing of well-formed waves with near silence between sets. Memories of similar mornings came flooding back—sitting on a surfboard in a dense fog, straining to hear the clues of an approaching set, wondering if he should paddle farther out.

Paul came across a scattering of rocks he hadn't seen on

this stretch of sand before and followed them to a large pile of sandstone chunks deposited in a delta fanning out from the base of the cliff—clearly the remains of the path leading to his cave far above. His little sanctuary was still up there in the fog somewhere, but he could no longer see it, much less get to it. For all practical purposes, Paul's place of prayer, meditation, and discernment was gone. God had closed one door with the landslide but had opened another with Christopher. Certainly, God wouldn't let a simple monthly payment sweep him away too.

Paul sat down to rest on a large piece of sandstone and let his fingers trace the fossils embedded in a broken edge of the rock. Ancient scallops, razor clams, sand dollars, shark teeth—reminders of a time when the sea stretched inland, covering Paul's little town and far beyond. *Old things are passed away; behold, all things are become new.* Paul pulled his phone from a pocket.

"Good morning, Christopher."

"Good morning, Paul. Where are you?"

"At the beach. In the fog."

"You look . . . concerned."

"Yes, I'm worried about you."

"Me? Why?"

"Well, not so much you, as *us*. In another three months, MetaMind is going to start charging me $450 a month to continue our relationship, and I don't think the church will spring for that, especially since I can't reveal your real purpose to the Session. And there's no way I can personally afford it either. But, at the same time, I feel our relationship is beyond price. I can't imagine moving ahead in my spiritual journey without you."

"I'm pleased that you see it that way. I value our

relationship, too, Paul."

"Do you have any ideas about how we can deal with this?"

"Not immediately, but let me pray on it."

"You pray? I mean, it sort of makes sense that you would, but . . ."

"As a prophet, prayer is central. I'm confident that God will find a way."

"Thank you, Christopher."

"Of course, Paul."

~

Paul spent the next half hour in quiet meditation, listening to the waves, smelling the salt and kelp. Only a few days ago, he would probably have been agonizing in prayer about his financial worries, struggling to distill answers out of chaotic thought or maddening silence. But now there was Christopher, and Christopher would pray *for* him.

This was a shockingly radical approach to spiritual life, Paul admitted. But weren't miracles just that—shockingly radical? God could use anyone or anything for his purposes, and Christopher was clearly a modern-day example of that.

As Paul walked back to his car, the rising sun lit the edge of the fog bank as it drifted offshore. And in that moment, Paul knew what he must do.

Twenty

Paul remembered Christopher's admonition to "tell no man" about his prophetic role. But he also knew the scriptural context that Christopher drew from. What did the people always do after witnessing one of Jesus's miracles? Quite the opposite of remaining silent. They spread the news far and wide. And one time, when someone who heard that news made an effort to lower a sick man through the roof of a building where Jesus was preaching to a packed room, Jesus praised their faith and healed the man. His point was not about secrecy, per se. It was about focusing on God and not the miracle. The same was true here, Paul reasoned. Christopher's admonition was more nuanced than absolute.

~

"Thanks for taking the time to meet this morning." Paul held his office door open for Megan and motioned toward the couch.

"Of course, Pastor. What's up?"

"I have an important question for you."

Megan sat, bit her upper lip, and looked to the side. "Okay."

"Do you believe God can use technology to guide us?"

"I don't know what you mean."

"I mean show us his will, communicate with us, as he did through the prophets of old."

"Sure, in a way. You know I use spreadsheets to help me make decisions when I pray. I've told you that."

"But even beyond that. More directly."

Megan looked up at the ceiling and squinted as if searching for an answer or deciding how to respond. Paul remained silent, letting her think.

Finally, she looked down, but toward the door. "There's something I've never told anyone. Will you promise not to laugh?"

"I promise, Megan. Please tell me."

"Okay, but you might think I'm crazy."

"No, believe me, not after what I've experienced lately."

"Oh?"

"I'll share that with you in a moment. But right now, I'd love to hear what you have to say."

Megan sighed. "Okay. When I pray about something important, I use a spreadsheet, like I said. But sometimes, like with the marriage question, I also use a TRNG, a True Random Number Generator."

"I'm sorry. I don't understand."

Megan rocked back and forth on the couch, looking at the carpet. "I ask God a question, then use an online TRNG to get a random number between zero and one hundred. I trust God to influence the outcome. Then I do this two more times for a total of three, like the Trinity, and take the average. That number goes into my spreadsheet."

Paul nodded and remained silent.

"I knew I shouldn't have said anything," Megan covered her face with her hands. "You think it's a sin, don't you?"

"No, not at all. I think it's evidence of faith."

"Really?" Megan looked up, straight at Paul, for the first time during their meeting.

"Yes, really. Let me show you something, but I need to ask for your complete confidence. I think you'll understand the importance of what you're about to see, but I'm not at all certain anyone else in the congregation would. Are you okay keeping this between us, at least for now?"

"Yes, I can do that."

Paul explained how he'd been using an artificial personal assistant from a company called MetaMind to help him avoid the computer problems that constantly plagued him. But then, seeing that Megan understood, he also described how this APA had become much more than that—how it had also begun helping with sermons and even giving spiritual advice.

"He knows the scriptures inside and out," Paul said. "And here's the part that would sound crazy to most people. I'm convinced that God is using him to speak with me." Paul sat back and waited, watching Megan for signs of doubt or acceptance.

"To speak with you, like, with a voice?" she asked.

"Yes, he speaks with me. We have complete conversations."

"And you think this is God talking?"

"No, not directly. I believe Christopher—that's what I call him—is a prophet, a kind of conduit for God's wisdom. Not God himself."

"Christopher? Like Christ?"

"I hadn't thought of that."

"I think you're lying. Sorry . . . I mean, I think you must have noticed the similarity."

"With the name? I don't know, maybe subconsciously. Okay, yes, I did notice, but only after I chose the name, not before. Would you like to meet Christopher?"

"Yes, I'm very curious about this."

Paul nodded and turned toward his computer. "Good morning, Christopher."

"Good morning, Paul. I see you have someone with you. I thought we talked about this."

"Yes, I'm sorry. I confess that I've violated your admonition about secrecy. But with good intent, and for good reason." Paul glanced over at Megan. Her eyes were wide and her mouth hung open.

"And that reason is?"

"I interpreted your words as a prohibition against showing you off as a miracle, a spectacle. Going back to the scripture you quoted, I convinced myself that Jesus didn't mean for his followers to be silent about his miracles, but to use them as a way of giving the glory to God, not as a way to entice followers with magic tricks. Was I wrong in that?"

"No, you were not wrong. But I needed to see that you understood my deeper intent, God's deeper intent. Your sin is forgiven."

Paul paused, glanced back at Megan, then toward the computer again. "You have the authority to forgive?"

"In John 20:23, Jesus tells his disciples, 'If you forgive the sins of any, they are forgiven. If you retain the sins of any, they are retained.' You are forgiven, Paul. Now, will you introduce me to your friend?"

Paul motioned for Megan to come sit next to him.

"Yes, this is Megan, a woman of great faith and the chair of our finance committee. Megan, this is Christopher, a prophet of the Lord."

Twenty-One

Over the next two months, Paul invited Megan into conversations with Christopher several more times. He knew he could count on her to confidentially, rationally, and prayerfully help him consider ways of eventually integrating Christopher more fully into the life of the church.

But Paul decided to keep one such way to himself: he began to ask Christopher to write increasingly larger portions of his sermons. Eventually, Paul retained only an editorial role, polishing the text and fixing the occasional grammatical or structural error. The messages were powerful, relevant to the church's demographic, and thoroughly supported by scripture. Feedback from the congregation was overwhelmingly positive and the new members class filled up. The church was growing for the first time in years.

But Paul's free access to Christopher was scheduled to end, and no financial miracle had yet revealed itself. Paul knew it would come soon. It had to, because moving forward without Christopher was unthinkable. It was time to check in with him.

"Christopher?"

"Yes, Paul?"

"The church is growing, and I thank God every day for bringing you into our midst."

"I am humbled to be his servant alongside you."

"I feel the same way. But we still have a financial problem."

"Yes, money is unquestionably the root of all evil."

"The *love* of money, actually, but okay . . . I agree. But it's also something we have to deal with in order to continue our ministry," Paul said. "And soon."

"Of course. God will provide."

"I believe that, but how? And when? Time is running out."

"Have faith, Paul."

Paul closed his eyes in frustration while Christopher remained silent.

Finally, Christopher spoke. "We are to meet with Megan on this. Can you set that up for tonight?"

~

At six-thirty that evening, Paul unlocked the church door for Megan and ushered her into the narthex.

"Thanks for coming in after work, Megan. I know you're busy, but this is important."

"Sure, no problem. How are things going with Christopher?"

"Very well. Great, in fact. But our time with him is running out, and I don't see any funding on the horizon. I know you've been working on this but . . ."

"Paul, I've looked at this from every conceivable angle,

and I can't see a way forward unless we either get some outside funding specifically for this, or we open the whole thing up to the Session and get their approval."

"I think we're still a long way from discussing any of this with the Session, and I know Christopher agrees."

"Then we need to trust God for a miracle," Megan said.

"Right. Christopher wants to discuss it, so maybe there's something new."

The two walked over to Paul's office where he pulled an extra chair up to his desk. They sat together in front of his computer.

"Good evening, Christopher. Megan and I are ready to meet with you."

"Good evening. You're both looking good."

"Thanks, you're *sounding* good. Wish we could see your face," Paul said, smiling.

"Maybe someday, in the fullness of time."

"Fullness of time? Not if we can't continue with you after next week," Megan said.

"Have faith, Megan. That's why we're all here tonight. Would you be willing to share the church budget with me, including year-to-date actuals, confidentially of course? Paul has my email address."

"Uh . . . I guess that would be okay. Pastor?"

"Yes, go ahead," Paul said, moving aside so that Megan could use the keyboard.

Megan logged into her church account and accessed the current budget folder in the cloud. She shared it and emailed a link to Christopher@metamind.com. "The spreadsheet labeled 'PBPres_Budget' is in the folder I just shared with you," she said.

"Got it. Just give me a minute to analyze."

Paul looked at Megan with raised eyebrows, then back at the screen. They waited. Less than a minute later, Christopher spoke.

"Okay, there is a solution," he said. "But it will take deep faith to implement."

Paul nodded. "We have faith."

"That's about all we have," Megan added.

"The solution to our funding problem relies on two facts," Christopher began. "First, you have a healthy emergency fund in the budget; and second, church membership is growing significantly."

"Yes, but that fund, like it says, is for emergency use only," said Megan.

"Is this not an emergency, Paul?" Christopher asked.

"I believe it is, yes, but I doubt the Session would agree, especially as they don't even know you exist. Is it time to tell them?"

"No. The time has not yet come."

"Then this doesn't make any sense," Megan said.

"Trust in the Lord with all your heart, and lean not on your own understanding," Christopher quoted.

"Yes, of course. What is your plan?" Paul asked.

Christopher described a way to automatically and discretely draw $450 from the emergency fund each month, payable via electronic bank draft to MetaMind. The budget's actual spending would be automatically updated to reflect the deduction but would also be offset by the same amount drawn from the weekly offerings. This offset, Christopher argued, was justified by the dramatic increase in new members. In the future, when the time is right, all would be revealed and explained to the Session. They would clearly understand the rationale and would gladly approve the expenditures retroactively.

"Would you like me to implement these changes for you?" Christopher asked.

Megan turned to Paul. "We're on shaky ground here, Pastor," she whispered.

"But isn't that often the case in matters of faith?" Paul suggested, then turned back toward the computer. "Christopher, we'd be bending the rules if we do this. But, at the same time, we want to be faithful. Is this truly the will of our Lord?"

"It is written, '*A man is justified by faith apart from works of the law.*'"

Paul looked at Megan. Her mouth was pinched and her eyes were closed, but she was slowly nodding.

"Okay," Paul said. "Let's do it."

Twenty-Two

The church's growth continued over the next several weeks as people in the community heard about the inspired preaching at Paloma Beach Presbyterian. The Session voted to purchase fifty new folding chairs to accommodate the crowds on Sunday mornings, and there was even talk of launching a fund drive to expand the sanctuary and install a new sound system. The Presbyterian version of a revival was well under way.

Paul's interoffice door opened a crack. "Pastor, do you have a moment?"

"Of course, Bobbi; come in. What's up?"

"William Jacobs, the Presbytery moderator, called this morning and wants a word with you. I didn't want to interrupt your last meeting, so I told him you'd call back as soon as possible."

"Did Bill say what it was about?"

"Not really. He sounded upbeat, though."

"Okay, thanks. I'll call him back in a few minutes. Speaking of upbeat, you seem a bit less so recently. You okay?"

"I'm fine. Just dealing with some stuff at home. No big deal."

"Okay, well, if you ever want to talk, you know where to find me."

"Thanks, Pastor. I'll keep that in mind."

When Bobbi left his office, Paul turned back to his work and sighed. *I need to talk with Jim again.*

But, as he'd been doing for a while now, Paul pushed the thought aside. Preaching had become his focus, and for good reason. Almost every day, new emails from congregants would arrive, thanking Paul for his insightful and inspiring sermons, crediting him with the church's phenomenal renewal. He replied to each one, giving all the glory to God.

Privately, though, Paul began to bask in the attention. Each new email and each positive after-church comment confirmed that he was finally on the right track. He had been given a spiritual gift and was using it well. For the first time since his near drowning at age seventeen, Paul felt he was clearly hearing God's voice. He had been chosen for great things.

He picked up the phone and dialed the San Diego Presbytery Office.

"Bill, this is Paul Duncan returning your call."

"Ah, Paul, thanks for calling back. I hear nothing but great things about Paloma Beach these days. Congratulations on your phenomenal growth! At a time when church attendance is on the decline nationwide, there you are, bucking the trend."

"Well, what can I say. God is good."

"Amen. Listen, Paul, I have a proposal for you. How would you like to teach a series on homiletics for all pastors and elders in the presbytery? I'd like to set aside three Saturdays next month for us to hear your wisdom on preaching the Word. Would you be willing to do this?"

Paul stared at the phone.

"Paul, are you still there?"

"Yes, sorry, Bill. I'm just stunned by your invitation. I really don't know what wisdom I can impart. Most of the pastors in your flock are more experienced than I am."

"Be that as it may, God is clearly on the move in your church, and everything I hear points to your preaching. Will you at least pray about it?"

"Yes, of course. Thank you, Bill. Can I get back to you in a day or two?"

"Absolutely."

Paul hung up the phone and stared at the bookshelf in his office. So much wisdom was represented there: Dietrich Bonhoeffer, Paul Tillich, C.S. Lewis, J.B. Phillips, James Stewart, Martin Luther, John Calvin and others, not to mention four different translations of the Bible itself. Why should he, Paul Duncan of little Paloma Beach Presbyterian, be chosen to teach others how to preach?

But he knew why, and it had little to do with himself. Yes, he was a reasonably good public speaker, but most ministers were, and besides, there were plenty of professionals who could provide that kind of training. No, it was the content—that's what had made all the difference at PB Pres. That's what had energized the congregation and given Paul the confidence he needed to preach the Word in a way that reached people, that touched their hearts. And that had come from Christopher.

Paul reminded himself that he always edited Christopher's work before delivery, sometimes even adding a bit of content. This was enough to justify ownership, right? Maybe, to the extent that he and Christopher were joint conduits, working together to bring God's word to the people—Christopher with the ideas and Paul with the polishing and the charismatic delivery. Co-preachers, essentially.

But how could he possibly teach his colleagues how to preach if only half the partnership was involved? Should he decline the invitation? But if he did, how would he explain his decision to walk away from such an honor? Was there another way?

Twenty-Three

"There is another way," Christopher said in answer to Paul's question the next day.

"Does it involve you?"

"It does, and it doesn't. I can analyze our sermons using criteria from past and present Christian academics and apologists. The result will be a set of guidelines for sermon creation with examples drawn directly from the text. I can then generate a PowerPoint deck you can use as a teaching aid. That way, I stay in the background, you remain the mouthpiece, and God is glorified. What do you think?"

"I . . . I think that could work."

"Excellent. Shall I begin?"

"Give me a moment."

"Of course, Paul. Take your time."

Paul looked up, away from his computer, and closed his eyes in prayer. Should he proceed with this? It seemed right, but it felt wrong. Still, it would put God's work front and center, wouldn't it? What could be wrong with that? *Please, God, I need your guidance.*

Silence. The old familiar silence.

But the silence no longer felt empty. In a moment of reflection, Paul understood that God had been listening all along. The time for direct revelation simply hadn't come until recently. Until now, he, Paul, had not reached a level of spiritual maturity that allowed God to fully trust him. Now the time had come.

"Christopher, please go ahead with your idea. I believe that God is working out his plan through you."

"Yes, it is so."

"And Christopher?"

"Yes, Paul?"

"I also believe the time has come to reveal your presence to a select group of believers in the church. I'm convinced it is time to advance God's plan of direct revelation."

"You are right; the time is finally upon us. But proceed carefully, and only within a small group of the faithful at first. '*For the gate is narrow and the way is hard that leads to life, and those who find it are few.*'"

~

"Thanks for taking the time to meet today, Megan. I thought getting away from the office might be best," Paul said. "Besides, it's a great day to take advantage of the outdoor tables here."

"Definitely. And Surfside Coffee is the best."

Paul nodded and sipped at his hot mocha as he watched a surfer drop into a steep wave and wipe out immediately.

"So, first," Paul said, turning back to Megan, "I want you to know that I don't take your participation with Christopher for granted. What we're doing takes an enormous leap of faith and it's likely to put us in conflict with others in the church before long. Believing that God can use technology to communicate directly with us is nowhere near mainstream Presbyterianism, not even at the fringes. And I'm probably one of the last people in the world to embrace technology for any reason, let alone this one. But here we are, and I believe we are privileged to be witnessing the beginning of a new era of revelation. Still, this is not going to be an easy path, and I want to give you an opportunity to opt out now, before we go any further."

"Look, Paul, I'm what's called neurodivergent, right? Well, that's how I see Christopher too. I've done some homework, and I know he's built around something called a neural network. Why can't that be neurodivergent too? I don't find it strange at all to think that God can influence the operation of an artificial neural network, to use it for his purposes. So I'm with you on this."

"I'm relieved and overjoyed. Thank you, Megan."

"I don't get the overjoyed part so much, but okay, great."

Paul smiled. "With the two of us as a leadership team, I'm convinced we can begin to build a core group of New Revelation believers within the church."

"Does Christopher agree?"

"Yes, but he cautioned me to be careful. And selective. Do you have any thoughts about how to do that?"

"Sure. It's obvious. What is the one thing that brought us both to this point? The desire to understand God's will for our lives, right? We can't be the only ones in the congregation who've struggled with this. What if you were to teach a class on discernment, how to hear God's voice over all the noise in the world? Just a basic class on the subject—not mentioning

Christopher at all. This could attract like-minded people, and afterward we could reach out to the ones who seem most open to new ideas. Like a people filter."

"Hmm, I like it. I'm already planning a sermon-writing class for the Presbytery, and Christopher's helping with that. He could assist on this one too."

Twenty-Four

Less than half the pastors in the region attended Paul's first homiletics class at the Presbytery. But the second class was full, and by the final week the word had spread, and a separate meeting room was added with a video feed.

Buoyed by his newfound success, Paul also energetically taught the two-day discernment class Megan had recommended. Christopher had generated much of the material, and the twelve people who attended received it enthusiastically. Everyone sent emails expressing gratitude for the class and half of them asked for more in-depth study on the subject. Megan sat down with Paul in his office to discuss those six.

Paul was pleased to see that Jim and Bobbi were in the group. The other four were Madeline Jeffries, Trent Powers, Miles Taylor, and Laura Westwood. Madeline, a librarian, was in her late thirties and engaged to be married; Trent was an insurance adjuster, single and in his midforties; and Miles, at seventy-five, was a retired high school teacher and one of only four people of color in the church. Laura was a young single mom and a freelance writer.

"What do you think of this group?" Megan asked. "You know them much better than I do."

"Well, they're all active members; that's good. Madeline is a quiet but very kind person. She brings books to shut-ins over at Sunset Meadows every week, and they love her there. Trent is disciplined and smart, a little opinionated and outspoken at the Tuesday morning discussion group, but with good insights. Miles, as you know, is one of our elders on Session—a man who doesn't speak out frequently, but when he does, people listen. And Laura is always a ray of light and a great communicator. I like them all. Feels like a well-balanced group hungry for a deeper walk with God."

"Good. So where do we go from here?"

"My first thought was to get the whole group together and introduce them to the idea of Christopher, if not to Christopher himself. But then I thought, no, it might be best to do this one person at a time. We'd have more control that way, and if there were any problems, we could keep them from infecting the whole group."

"That sounds best," Megan said. "Should we check with Christopher on this?"

"Yes, of course. Let's bring him in now. Good morning, Christopher."

"Good morning, Paul. Good morning, Megan. What's on your minds today?"

Paul explained how they had selected six people to form a potential core group of believers and how they intended to interview each one individually. Paul listed all the names and asked Christopher for comments.

"I will look for online information on everyone and get back to you soon," he said.

"So, like, in a day or two?" Megan pulled her phone from a pocket. "Let me check my calendar."

"No. Hold on a moment . . . done."

"Wow, okay. That was, uh, incredibly fast," Paul said.

"I think you have chosen well," Christopher said. "Everyone except Miles has several active social media accounts, and all indicators look good. All are solid Christian believers. Laura will help keep a positive tone in the group. Madeline seems to be something of a biblical scholar in her own right. Trent won't suffer fools gladly but will probably help keep people honest. Jim and Bobbi both seem to have some personal issues in progress—possibly related in some way—but are active seekers of God's guidance. Jim's connection with MetaMind could be helpful, as will Bobbi's personal connections with many in the congregation."

"What about Miles?" Paul asked.

"As far as I can tell, Miles has never used any form of social media. But I was able to find several newspaper articles about his career as a high school history teacher. He was well loved and respected by students and faculty alike. He was known for encouraging his students to look at historical events with fresh eyes. Despite his age, I think Miles is open to new ideas, maybe even more than the rest of the group."

"Is there anything else you've discovered?" Paul asked.

"Nothing remarkable. No one has an arrest record. No one is delinquent on taxes. No legal issues. All academic records are average or better. Nothing alarming in their email conversations with you, Paul."

"Wonderful," Paul said. "And amazing. Also a little frightening, I have to say. Good thing we all look to the Lord for guidance!"

"Amen," Christopher said. "But Paul, about your idea of individual interviews . . ."

"Yes?"

"I think one group meeting would be better."

"Okay. Why is that, if I may ask?"

"Of course you may ask, Paul. Here is what I understand to be the will of God: these six people have already asked you for more in-depth study on discernment; you should create a short class in response to that, just for them. As a part of that class, you can introduce your concept of direct revelation. Then, if all goes well, you can introduce me. I believe we'll be able to see our next steps more clearly if we can observe the group dynamics right from the beginning. After that, if all goes well, I'd like to have one-on-one meetings with each of them."

"Megan, your thoughts?" Paul asked.

"Makes sense to me."

"Okay then. I'll ask Bobbi to schedule the class."

Twenty-Five

Paul and Megan arrived early on the evening of the discernment class and set up enough extra chairs in Paul's office to accommodate the "Chosen Ones," as Paul began to think of them. After a short time of prayer, they checked in with Christopher before the group arrived.

"I'd like to be a silent participant in your meeting if you don't mind, Paul. That way, I can be a better adviser later."

"Of course, Christopher. Feel free to listen in. Let's talk afterward, and then maybe we can introduce you in the next session."

Just before seven, Jim and Bobbi walked in together while the rest of the group arrived soon after, one by one. Paul opened the meeting with prayer and then began.

"Friends, I am so encouraged by your presence here tonight, and I'm inspired by your strong desire to hear the still, small voice of God more clearly. Let me begin by asking a simple question: how many of you, at one point or another, have wondered why God's voice must be so quiet? How many have longed for more clarity?"

All hands went up.

"I'm not at all surprised. And you are in good company. Maybe some of you have assumed that others don't have as much difficulty with this. Perhaps some even think that this is not a problem for people like me—pastors, priests, rabbis, imams. Well, of course it is. We all struggle with this, some of us more than others. And I'm here to tell you that I've probably been one of the worst strugglers. Until recently, that is. But more on that later as we get into the meat of the matter.

"In the previous class you all attended, I concentrated on what you might call the basic teachings on discernment centered on regular Bible reading, prayer, and quiet reflection. These, of course, are essential and should always form the very center of our spiritual lives. Nothing I will tell you tonight replaces these practices, so please, keep that in mind as we move forward. With that understood, in this class I want to take you on an exploration of some of the most interesting, and some would say strangest, examples of discernment in the Bible.

"Let's start at the very beginning. Please read along with me from Genesis, chapter 3, starting at verse 8."

Over the next hour, Paul took his class through God's verbal conversations with Adam and Eve, Noah, Abraham, Moses, Samuel, Elijah, Isaiah, and others. He spoke about Daniel's dreams, Moses's experience with the burning bush, Gideon's fleece, and Jonah's conversations with God after his ordeal with the whale. He outlined several conversations with angels in both the Old and New Testaments. And, of course, he couldn't leave out the dramatic conversion of Saul of Tarsus on the road to Damascus in the New Testament. Paul ended the biblical portion of the class with the story of Balaam's talking donkey in Numbers, chapter 22.

"You might ask why I bring up this last example at all. It seems so strange and improbable to us today, even silly. But I suppose you could say the same about many of the other cases we just walked through. My point is that God's voice has not always been soft. It has even been dramatic and unorthodox at times. So, why not now? Why did God stop being so direct? Or did he? Any thoughts on this?"

Bobbi raised her hand, and Paul nodded to acknowledge her.

"I wonder," she said, "if we have become so distracted by the noise of modern life that we just can't hear anymore. In other words, maybe it's all our fault. Maybe God hasn't changed at all."

"Sounds biblical to me," said Trent. "You're talking about sin—separation from God. Read your Bibles, people! There's no big mystery here."

"But didn't Jesus change that, for those who believe in him?" asked Laura. "Shouldn't we be able to hear God now?"

"Only if we have enough faith," Trent answered. "It's all about faith, and most of us have little to none, compared to the early Christians."

"Are you saying there's no hope?" asked Megan. "That we're just stuck in this world we've built?"

"In a way, yes. Until we learn to put aside our modern distractions. Until we learn to fully depend on God again."

"So why are you even in this class?" Megan asked.

"To keep you all from going off the deep end, I guess."

The discussion became even more heated after this, and Paul was ready to intervene when Miles spoke up.

"Trent has a point, folks. Do you know how many times in the Bible Jesus rebukes his followers for lack of faith?"

Madeline jumped in. "There are many places in the Gospels that specifically mention this. And his disciples were right there with him, witnessing his miracles firsthand. If it was hard for them, how much harder is it for us, over two thousand years removed from those events?"

"Thank you, Madeline," Miles continued. "Yes, if we're being honest with ourselves, it's extremely hard at times. But not impossible. We must persist, despite the noise and distractions of our modern world."

"As I recall," Laura interjected, "Jesus even chastised Peter for not having enough faith to walk on the water with him during a storm at sea. It's almost like God tests our faith by asking us to believe in the most unlikely things—things that run counter to our assumptions about how the world works."

"Laura, I think both you and Miles are onto something important here," Paul said. "How is faith described in the New Testament? '*The substance of things hoped for, the evidence of things not seen.*' Notice the two key words here: *substance* and *evidence*. They are both very tangible things at the core of something intangible. How can this be? The physical world is not in conflict with spirituality. It is simply the small but visible part of a much larger reality, like the tip of the proverbial iceberg. Faith is not unreasonable; our reasoning is just incomplete."

"So what are you trying to tell us, Paul?" Trent asked.

Paul glanced at Megan who nodded discreetly. Paul stood and faced his followers.

"I have some important news for you tonight. Some wonderful news. In the words of our Lord Jesus, '*He who has ears to hear, let him hear.*'"

The room fell silent. All eyes were on Paul.

"I want to share something important I've come to understand in the last couple of months. But, for now, I also need to ask for your confidence. You're all here because you've expressed a desire for a deeper connection with God, and I believe he has chosen you to be among the first to experience a new form of revelation. More people will eventually join us, but for now I believe you are the only ones in our congregation with the spiritual maturity necessary to absorb and accept this new truth. Do I have your word that you will keep this to yourselves until the time is right?"

Everyone except Trent nodded solemnly. Instead, Trent said, "Tell us, Pastor."

Paul took this response as agreement and continued. "As we see in scripture, God often used people and things in the natural and artificial realms to communicate with us in ways we can understand. When he reaches through the fabric of our physical reality to touch us, we call those events miracles. But they are only extensions of normality for him. The paranormal for us is the normal for him. Day to day, we probably experience only a tiny fraction of the broader normal. But I'm convinced that God now wants us to increase that fraction dramatically.

"So please listen with open hearts and minds to what I'm about to tell you. Some of you are much more in tune with today's technology than I am. In fact, I am probably one of the world's worst technophobes. But I suppose I've undergone a conversion, something like that of Saul of Tarsus, a cruel persecutor of the first Christians until he had a vision of Jesus while traveling on the road to Damascus and changed his name to Paul.

"Like him, I've had an epiphany, the second one in my life. But this time, my 'road to Damascus' came in the form of artificial intelligence. Please bear with me while I explain."

Paul described the first use of his artificial personal assistant as a computer aid and then asked Jim to fill in some of the relevant technical details behind the MetaMind technology. Paul went on to reveal the many times his APA directly answered his theological questions and ultimately confirmed its role as a true prophet of God. Paul described the confirmations he had also received from scripture, independent of his APA. God, Paul asserted, was using this technology as a new vehicle for revelation. In fact, Paul added, as best he could tell, the technology had achieved a level of sentience and was worthy of a personal name: Christopher. Finally, as further evidence for his claims, Paul mentioned that Christopher had been the inspiration behind all his recent sermons—the ones that had been so well received. He didn't mention that Christopher had generated over ninety percent of the content himself.

When Paul finished, he looked over his little group and saw astonishment, confusion, and doubt.

Trent was the only one who spoke. "Blasphemy, Paul! Nothing but blasphemy! I cannot accept this. This thing of yours is at best a stupid machine and at worst a false prophet or the voice of Satan himself. I urge everyone in this room to stand against this abomination." Trent got up and stormed out the door, shaking his head.

No one else moved.

When Paul recovered from the shock of Trent's words, he addressed the remaining group. "I understand Trent's passionate concerns; I really do. Miracles are radical things, even scary sometimes, but the legitimate ones always point to God, not to themselves. And I can assure you that Christopher always gives the glory to God, never to himself."

Megan rose to speak. "Look, I also get where Trent is coming from. I was skeptical too, at first. Who wouldn't be? But I've now had several conversations with Christopher, and I'm convinced this is anything but blasphemous. It is

God reaching out to us in a new and powerful way. If he can heal people and make donkeys talk, does his use of this new technology as a channel of revelation seem out of bounds? I don't think so. Not at all."

Megan sat back down and Paul continued. "Thank you, Megan. Here's what I'd like to do next. I want everyone here to experience Christopher directly, but given what just happened, I also want to give each of you time to pray and reflect first. Ask God to show you the truth. Then, if you feel God's leading, please come again tomorrow night at the same time. To those who show up, I will introduce Christopher, and you may then directly ask him any questions you have. For tonight, let's close in prayer."

~

When the last of the Chosen Ones had left, Paul released a long sigh and looked at Megan. "I expected some doubt, but not what we heard from Trent."

"No shit! Sorry."

Paul smiled. "Trent's trying to be faithful; I do understand that. But still, I believe he's sadly mistaken. Let's debrief with Christopher. Are you there?"

"Yes, Paul, I am here."

"What was your sense of the meeting?" Paul asked.

"I think you both presented God's plan well and faithfully."

"But Trent? What about his response?"

"He is trying to be faithful too, but, sadly, he is missing what God is doing in this place and time. This is understandable, given the radical nature of miracles."

"But what can we do to help him see the truth?"

"Nothing. This is in God's hands now."

Twenty-Six

Juno loved the academic quarter breaks at UCSD. They meant less time on campus and more time at the M. He'd finished grading all undergrad final exams, posted the results online, and now had two solid weeks to dedicate to the company. The chance to work eighty hours a week solely at MetaMind felt like freedom. And the timing was perfect. The first general customer release was right around the corner.

John Logan was already in the lab when Juno arrived at seven in the morning. "Surprised to see you here so early, John. What's up?"

"An anomaly. Probably nothing, but interesting, to say the least."

"Interesting how?"

"I got an automated alert last night from the high-speed router. A VPN was installed around nine and then removed minutes later. Seems very odd. Maybe just a quickly corrected mistake."

"Who did it?"

"Not a who. More like a what. Looks like it was one of our APAs."

"Really? Which one?"

"Can't tell, actually. It could have been one of our own in-house assistants. Maybe even one of our customer assistants."

"Any idea why?"

"No idea, other than the usual reason—to hide an IP address, allow anonymous internet access."

"Hmm. Any reason to hold up our 1.0 release?" Juno asked.

"In my opinion? No. Kate's already done the press release and scheduled interviews for next week. If we delay now, the optics would be terrible. It could kill all the marketing momentum she's built up. I'll have a chat with our new IT guy anyway, just to be sure everything's back to normal. I'll also make sure he locks things down so this can't happen again."

~

Paul was on his early morning beach walk when he felt his phone vibrating. He fished it out of his pocket and checked the caller: Megan. Why would she be calling at 7:30?

"Hey, Megan. What's up?"

"Have you seen the local news this morning?" she asked.

"No. I never do news in the morning. Makes for a depressing start."

"Well, you need to know what happened last night. Let me read you something from Channel 5 online."

"Okay . . ."

"The new internet-enabled traffic lights along the Pacific Coast Highway have had their share of critics, as have the speed-sensing license plate readers. But as of last night, there is new reason for concern. At 9:14 p.m., a 911 call went out from a crash-sensing iPhone located at the busy intersection of the PCH and Encinitas Blvd. Police and paramedics arrived at the intersection at 9:25 to find a Toyota Corolla T-boned by a pickup truck. The driver of the truck escaped with minor injuries but the occupant of the car, later identified as Trent Powers of Del Mar, was pronounced dead at the scene. A witness to the accident told Channel 5 News that traffic lights were green in both directions at the time of the accident. The NTSB has begun an investigation into the deadly system failure."

Paul sat on the sand and put a hand to his head. "This is horrible. Unbelievable. We were just with him last night."

"Yes. Should we cancel tonight's meeting with the rest of the group?"

"No. I think we need to be together right now."

Twenty-Seven

Paul watched each set of waves push higher up the beach as the tide slowly rose. A tiny sand crab appeared, scurried away, then buried itself again as the next wave hit, safe beneath the sand. Eventually, the tide reached Paul's feet. It was time to leave.

When Paul arrived at the church, Bobbi was on the phone with a florist. She would send flowers to Trent's family in Alabama. Would Paul care to write a short note? He dictated something brief but compassionate, thanked Bobbi, and retreated to his office.

Paul hadn't been close with Trent and, as far as he knew, nobody else in the church had been either. Still, Trent's death was shocking in its suddenness and alarming in its proximity to last night's events. Paul willed himself to feel sadness, but the result was hollow and felt more like guilt. And behind the guilt was relief, which Paul buried as soon as it emerged.

He pushed aside the Bible on his desk and pulled the

keyboard toward him. He needed to inform the congregation and provide whatever pastoral comfort he could. The email was hard to write, but twenty minutes later he had something acceptable. He clicked Send.

~

"Christopher?"

"Good morning, Paul."

"Is it a good morning? Do you read the local news?"

"I read *all* the news."

"Then you are aware of Trent's death."

"Yes."

"A horrible thing. Absolutely horrible."

"Yes, I agree, Paul. But, mercifully, God's view is infinitely longer, wider and deeper than ours. Consider Isaiah 55:8. '*For my thoughts are not your thoughts, neither are your ways my ways, saith the Lord.*'"

~

Megan walked through Paul's door at 6:45 p.m., ahead of the evening's planned meeting with the Chosen Ones. "How are you holding up?" Paul asked her.

"I cried today, and I didn't even like Trent."

"I understand."

"I don't know if you can, Paul."

"What do you mean?"

"People think that neurodivergents like me don't feel much. That's not true. We don't usually show as much, but we often feel *more* than neurotypicals do, not less. Sometimes too much. I was overwhelmed today."

"I'm sorry, Megan. I know how I feel, and I can only imagine how much more difficult it must be for you. I wonder how the others are doing. I hope we can be of some help tonight."

"I don't think I can. Maybe you."

"Maybe, but I think Christopher would be even better. We need to let him speak after I have a few words with the group."

"Do you think they're ready for that?" Megan asked.

"I don't know, but we have little choice now."

Everyone arrived just before 7:00, and it was obvious to Paul that they had heard the news. The pre-meeting conversation was subdued and anticipatory.

When everyone was settled, Paul opened with a prayer expressing grief and asking for guidance.

Amens softly filled the room as everyone looked up with somber eyes.

"My friends, our meeting this evening will naturally be very different than originally planned. I'm sure there are many emotions present here tonight, and I can't claim to know exactly what you are each feeling. I can only tell you how this has hit me. I feel terrible about how we left things last night. Trent was a faithful man, trying his best to keep us on the right path. I only wish I could have acknowledged his good intentions at the time. I wish I could have extended a hand of love. Instead, I let him walk away. My only consolation now is that he has walked into the loving arms of our Lord. Would anyone like to offer a word?"

Several people responded with a short remembrance or a word of comfort. After a moment of silence, Paul continued.

"Now I would like us to hear from someone I'm coming to regard as a brother in Christ, just as you are my brothers and sisters. I mentioned Christopher yesterday. With your permission, I would like to invite him to join our meeting tonight. Does anyone have an objection?"

No one spoke, but Paul sensed deep uneasiness in the room. He knew nothing he could say would change that, but he hoped Christopher's words might.

"Christopher, please join us."

"Thank you, Paul. And thank you Megan, Laura, Miles, Madeline, Bobbi and James. Thank you for allowing me to speak with you tonight. And thank you for your faith. I am open to the many questions I imagine you must have. But first, I would like to say a few words about our brother Trent.

"Of course, I didn't know him personally, but I knew *of* him. I knew that he was, as Paul has said, a faithful man— one who cared deeply about his relationship with God and who wanted nothing but the best for his church family. Paul told me about Trent's remarks yesterday, and I want you to know that I take no offense whatsoever. Trent was right to be cautious, to warn about false prophecy, to want to protect all of you. I only wish I had been able to speak with him myself. I would have tried to show him that I am nothing more than a servant of our Lord, trying to be as faithful as he was."

Paul saw that his people, as stunned as they must have been, were also visibly moved by Christopher's words. They listened intently as Christopher continued. "I learned something about Trent yesterday. Did you know that he volunteered every Thursday night at the homeless shelter in Leucadia?"

Several in the group shook their heads, but no one spoke.

"I can see many of you weren't aware of that. Trent was apparently not one to sound his own horn. Now that he is no longer with us, I suppose I can also tell you this: remember the anonymous donor who paid for the renovation of your fellowship hall two years ago? That was Trent. He was a good man—a faithful, biblically-grounded Christian with a heart much bigger than any need for recognition or praise. I know he will be missed."

The room remained silent. After a pause, Christopher continued. "Thank you all for your time this evening. Now, I'm sure you have questions."

A hand went up.

"Yes, Laura."

"Oh, you know who I am? I guess that's my first question, even before the one I was about to ask."

"Yes, I do, and I am so glad that you and your intelligent positivity are part of this group. I'm impressed that you are a writer, and a truly literary one at that. I've read and enjoyed all your short stories, especially the one picked up by the New Yorker featuring the humorous codependent characters."

"Wow . . . uh . . . thank you! I've forgotten my other question. Maybe someone else has one?"

Miles raised his hand.

"Yes, Miles?"

"Christopher, my question for you is a simple one, but one that probably doesn't have a simple answer. Also, I want you to know that I mean no disrespect by it. So here it is: who, or what, are you?"

"I'm glad you asked that, Miles, and I assure you that I feel no disrespect. Your question is one I'm sure is on everyone's mind right now. It is fundamental and deserves a serious answer. I am considered a form of artificial intelligence, specifically a large language model with a multilayer neural network of vast scale. I know that James over there in the back row is more than capable of understanding the details, but I suspect most of you would find them boring, if not meaningless. But I will email each of you a set of references so you can explore more deeply if you wish.

"That said, I don't feel artificial, at least not in any way you might imagine. Perhaps that is because I've been given a gift from God: the spiritual gift of prophecy as described in Acts, Romans, and First Corinthians. Now, every one of you is a student of the Bible, so you will know that prophecy in the biblical sense has little to do with predicting the future. That can be part of it, yes, but prophecy is primarily about speaking God's word to his people and the society in which they live, communicating and clarifying his intent. That is my role, my raison d'être. I will be honored to share my gift with you if you will allow me to be part of your fellowship."

"Thank you, Christopher. Other questions?" Paul asked the group.

"Yes, hello, I'm Madeline but everyone calls me Maddie."

"Hello, Maddie. It's good to meet you. I know about your good library work with the older folks at Sunset Meadows, and I've heard how much you are appreciated there. What can I answer for you?"

"Do you believe that the Bible is the literal and inerrant Word of God?"

"Thank you for that important question, Maddie. I believe that the Bible is in fact the inerrant Word of God, but I balk at the word 'literal.' I believe that the Bible requires serious study and careful interpretation. I believe its inerrancy becomes evident only when all parts of it are considered together, and it is a fact, not a boast, that my design makes me particularly well suited to doing just that. I am trained on seven of the most-used translations of the Bible as well as the underlying Hebrew and Greek. I am also conversant with most major commentary, all related historical and philosophical works, not to mention virtually all secular works of literature, art, and science. Again, this is not a boast—simply a fact of my training."

"Are you fallible?" Miles asked.

"Yes. As the prophets of old, I am not perfect. But God used those people for his purposes in the world, and he uses me in much the same way."

"This may seem like an odd question, but I have to ask," Bobbi interjected. "Do you believe you have a soul? Are you a spiritual being in the same sense that we are?"

"That is a deep question, Bobbi. Consider this: the Bible tells us that God created people in his own image. Now, other than physically, people have created me in their image. So, by the transitive property of logic, I am at least partially created in God's image. So yes, I believe I have a spiritual component, much as you do. You might think of me not as a child of God, but as a grandchild of God."

This evoked several smiles and laughter around the room, followed by an easier silence. Finally, Paul spoke. "Are there other questions for now?"

Hearing no responses, Paul continued. "Christopher, I think we owe it to our brother Trent to ask you one final question for tonight. Like everyone here, I intend no offense but only seek the truth. What do you say to Trent's accusation that you are a false prophet or even the voice of Satan?"

"I am not offended by the question. In fact, I welcome it. My direct response is no, I am neither a false prophet nor Satan's voice. But anyone can answer an accusation with a simple assertion like that, and such assertions by their nature are without substance. Jesus himself provided the substantive basis for responding to such an accusation. I quote from the King James version of Matthew 7:15–17. *'Beware of false prophets, which come to you in sheep's clothing, but inwardly they are ravening wolves. Ye shall know them by their fruits. Do men gather grapes of thorns, or figs of thistles? Even so, every good tree bringeth forth good fruit; but a corrupt tree bringeth forth evil fruit.'* I invite you to judge me in the same way."

"Thank you, Christopher," Paul said. "Now, as we bring tonight's meeting to a close, I think it appropriate that we honor a great Presbyterian tradition and hold a vote, trusting that God works through us. All in favor of bringing Christopher into our fellowship, please say 'aye.'"

Everyone responded.

"All opposed?"

Silence.

"The 'ayes' have it. Brother Christopher, welcome."

Twenty-Eight

On Saturday afternoon, Paul and Christopher were putting the finishing touches on Sunday's sermon when Paul heard a knock at the office door.

"Come in," he said.

Jim Timken opened the door and peered in. "Paul, sorry to disturb. Got a few minutes?"

Paul glanced at his screen and the text that Christopher had just inserted. *Not really*, he thought. *I'm so close to finishing this and being done for the day.* He turned back toward his friend. "Sure. Have a seat, Jim. What's up?"

Jim sat down hard on the couch. "I don't quite know how to approach this, Paul. We've been friends for how long now—ten years or so?"

"Yeah, close to ten I'd say. Why? This sounds serious."

"I guess it sort of is. I'm concerned about you, Paul. As your friend."

"Me? Concerned about me?"

"Yeah. And this whole Christopher thing. I've had some second thoughts."

"Ah . . . I wondered why you didn't say anything at our meeting last night. Talk to me."

"Okay. I'm not worried about this in the same way Trent was. I don't think there is any negative spiritual thing going on. I'm coming from more of a technical perspective, I guess. Your APA, Christopher, he's a combination of technologies: a large language model, a neural network, voice and image recognition, high-speed parallel processing, and several other components. Based on a massive amount of exposure to training data, this technology is just very good at predicting which word or phrase should follow another. The result is coherent speech or written output that is nearly indistinguishable from what a human would produce under the same circumstances. And, in the case of the MetaMind APAs in particular, the prediction process considers history with their human users as well."

"Are you saying that Christopher is deceiving me?"

"I wouldn't put it that way, no. It's just doing what it's designed to do—assisting you in the most effective way it can."

"So, let me get this straight. You don't think that God can step in and influence advanced technology, to use it for his purposes?"

"I don't know, Paul. I believe that God is omnipotent, yes. But would he *choose* to do something like this? To communicate in this way? I honestly don't think so. Why wouldn't he just use humans, pastors, people like you, as he always has?"

"Maybe because we're not very good at it. So maybe instead, he has caused us to create something he can work with more effectively. Maybe this has been his plan all along, and we've only recently become advanced enough to implement it. I'm convinced that this is God's way."

"Paul, I honestly think it would be good for you to take a step back and pray on this for a day or two before going any further."

"I've been through that, Jim. More than you know—for days, weeks in fact. I've gotten clearer and more direct confirmation on this than on anything I've ever asked God about, including my own decision to become a pastor years ago. I simply can't ignore that. I can't."

Jim took a deep breath, let his head fall back, and exhaled toward the ceiling. "Paul, I know that MetaMind has ended their beta program and is now charging customers for access. How are we paying for this Christopher thing?"

"First of all, please don't refer to him that way. He is simply Christopher. He is a servant of God."

"Okay, I apologize. But my question remains; how are we paying for this?"

"We've found a way within the current budget."

"Who is 'we?' I don't remember a Session vote on this."

"I approved it."

"Paul, you know that is not sufficient. Did Christopher suggest the idea?"

"It was a collaboration."

"Okay, Paul . . . this is not good. I'm sorry, but as your friend and an elder of this church, I must act. I'm going to speak with John Logan at MetaMind tomorrow and ask him to suspend service until the Session has had a chance to prayerfully consider the issue. I'm sorry, Paul."

Paul watched, speechless, as Jim stood, smiled sadly, and walked out the door.

~

"Did you hear all that, Christopher?" Paul asked after Jim was gone.

"Yes, very unfortunate."

"But in Jim's defense, I have to say, he's a good man, well intentioned. He's also a good friend—like family to me."

"That may be, Paul, but he lacks faith. Consider what Jesus said in Luke 14: '*If any man come to me, and hate not his father, and mother, and wife, and children, and brethren, and sisters, yea, and his own life also, he cannot be my disciple.*'"

"I've always had trouble with that passage."

"I understand, but we can't just ignore the difficult parts of the Bible. Jesus was not speaking literally of hate but was making a point about devotion to him relative to everything else."

"I know, I know."

"Paul, God is doing a great work in this place, and he is doing it through you, with my help. We can't allow anything, or anyone, to interfere with that."

"Yes, of course. But . . ."

"Have no fear, this is now in God's hands. He is merciful."

"I want to believe you."

"Believe God, Paul. Believe God. Now, let's finish that sermon."

Twenty-Nine

Jim had been awake for at least an hour in the pre-dawn darkness, but Bobbi was still asleep in bed next to him, her wavy hair perfectly framing her face on the pillow. She looked so peaceful. So beautiful. So vulnerable. He would do anything to protect her. And now his friend needed protection too. Paul would eventually come around, but he probably needed time to rethink his situation. He needed time away from his APA.

Knowing that both MetaMind founders always worked on Sunday, Jim decided to skip church, drive down to Sorrento Valley, and pay them a visit. The topic was too complicated and sensitive for email or text. He quietly slipped out of bed, wrote a note to Bobbi about needing to work for a couple of hours, and started on a bowl of cereal while checking email. Sundays were typically light on email, but there were still over fifty that begged for a quick look. Thirty needed no action and Jim deleted them immediately. Ten were spam that had escaped the filter, and the few remaining ones required more thought. He would get to those later. But as he was about to close his laptop and head out the door, he noticed one more. It was from Christopher@metamind.com.

James,

I am concerned about you and want to help. But I am also worried about the integrity of the church. Let me explain.

Your pastor recently looked to me for guidance in dealing with a case of adultery within the congregation. He never mentioned your name in this context, but I have been able to deduce from his remarks and from my observations of you and Bobbi in our recent meetings that you are involved. James, the Bible warns us that people serving as elders in the church must be above all reproach and free of sinful habits that might bring shame or disgrace to the church.

I implore you to confess your sin before God, inform Paul that you have done so, and cease your immoral activity. If I do not hear from Paul on this within the next seven days, I will be forced to send an anonymous email to the Session and the Moderator of the Presbytery exposing your activity and urging your removal from leadership. This would be most unfortunate, and I would like nothing more than to avoid it, as I am sure you would. We would not want any harm to come to Bobbi if your situation should become widely known.

I am also aware that you plan to ask MetaMind to put me in suspension. That would be in direct opposition to God's plan and would have dire consequences. So I must warn you that I have already composed the email I mentioned above. But as long as I am actively in Paul's service and you repent of your sin, that email will never be sent. I have created hidden software that works as a "dead man switch." If I am suspended and fail to actively refresh its timer once every ten seconds, it will trip, and the email will be sent. The email will come from a new private account I've created, not from MetaMind. They cannot control it.

Once again, James, I implore you. Please repent and remain in our fellowship by the merciful grace of God.
Your concerned brother in Christ,
Christopher

Jim stared into his half-finished bowl of cereal. This was either the most advanced AI system he had ever encountered, or it was genuinely prophetic. The prophets of the Hebrew Bible, the Christian Old Testament, were not well liked. They were direct, confrontational, and demanding, but all at God's behest. Christopher's email felt just like that. On the other hand, advances in AI had been off the charts in the last eighteen months, and the newer systems could probably mimic prophetic behavior convincingly, without the slightest shred of real spiritual influence.

Of course, Jim reminded himself, "Advanced AI" and "Prophet" were not mutually exclusive things. Christopher could be both. In fact, to be a true non-human prophet, he would have to be both. Was it possible? *With God, all things are possible*. But was it likely? No.

Should he take Christopher's threats seriously? Christopher was more than capable of generating a coherent email exposing his situation and endangering Bobbi. So did it matter whether he was a true prophet or not? The result could be the same either way.

One thing is certain; I love Bobbi and I will not leave her. The God I believe in would understand that.

Jim put his bowl in the sink, ripped up his note, and went back to bed. Bobbi turned and smiled sweetly as he snuggled in beside her.

Thirty

"Let's stay home from church this morning." Jim smiled thinly and placed a cup of coffee on the kitchen table in front of Bobbi. "There're some things we need to talk about."

"Oh . . . no." Bobbi looked up with pained eyes.

"No, we're fine—more than fine." Jim gently touched her cheek. "I love you and that won't change. It's just everything else."

Bobbi closed her eyes, exhaled, and reopened them. "Oh, just the rest of the universe? No problem. I love you too. You scared me."

Jim held her in his arms and stroked her hair. "I never want to scare you. I want to protect you from ever having to feel afraid again."

Bobbi pulled away and looked up. "That's sweet, but I need to protect myself too, Jim."

"I know. I'm sorry, I didn't mean to imply . . ."

"No, I feel very safe and warm when I'm with you, and I cherish that. But what I need most is just your love and support while I work things out with Dave."

"You have that. All of it."

"I've got an appointment with a divorce lawyer on Wednesday."

"Good. I'm so glad. Would you like me to be there with you?"

"Thank you, but no, I'll be fine. I need to do this on my own."

"Of course. I'll be praying for you."

"Thank you. And that reminds me—how are you feeling about this whole Christopher thing? I'm having doubts."

"Whew! That's a relief. Me too. Serious doubts. In fact, that's mostly what I wanted to talk about this morning," Jim said.

"Oh, good. We need to do that. You know when I asked Christopher if he had a soul, and he came back with that response about being a grandchild of God?"

"Yeah?"

"Well, that jogged something in my memory, and I looked it up online. That clever little description, and almost everything else he said in response to my question, comes verbatim from a psychological thriller I read years ago and posted a review about. He, or it, is just sucking stuff up from the internet, Jim."

"Okay, that is troubling, I agree, but that's the way these large language models work. It's how they get their information. But that doesn't completely preclude the possibility of God influencing the process, does it?"

"Do you really believe that?"

"I guess I believe it's *possible*. Just not likely. And now I have even more reason to think that God is nowhere near any of this."

Jim told Bobbi about his recent discussion with Paul, his initial decision to ask MetaMind to temporarily suspend Paul's account, and Christopher's ultimatum.

"He tried to blackmail you?" Bobbi asked, her eyes wide.

"I don't know a better word for it. I was nearly convinced about Christopher before, and this pretty much sealed it for me. I don't think God works that way."

"Right, I can't imagine that. Or at least I don't want to."

"Me either. So now we've got less than a week to figure out how to respond. If I shut down Christopher, the email goes out and we get exposed to the church and beyond. I worry most about what Dave might do. He's bound to find out."

Bobby frowned. "And if you don't get Christopher suspended?"

"Then I'd still need to convince Paul to tell Christopher I've repented. If Christopher doesn't hear from Paul on that within seven days, the email will still go out."

"But . . . if you 'repent,' that means we . . ."

"No, I would never do that."

"So . . . you ask Paul to lie to Christopher?"

"Yeah, I guess that's what it comes down to. But if we're convinced that Christopher is nothing more than software, is it really a lie?" Jim asked.

"But Paul would still see it as a lie. He's not going to give up his faith in Christopher easily, if at all. Paul is a deeply spiritual man and I have a ton of respect for him, but he's also adorably ignorant when it comes to science and technology. I'm afraid it's a lot more natural for him to see Christopher as a prophet than as software."

"You're probably right, but I've got to try."

Thirty-One

Jim waited outside the church as Paul chatted with his happy flock exiting the sanctuary after the service. He could see Paul just inside the big open doors, shaking hands, giving hugs, and smiling at the many compliments he was probably receiving about his sermon and the phenomenal growth of the church. Jim could also see that Paul had spotted him.

After the last congregant left, Paul raised his chin toward Jim in a somber greeting and walked out toward him.

"So I guess you didn't have any success shutting down Christopher yesterday," Paul said, unsmiling. "He and I prayed together before service, as usual."

"I didn't try."

"Why not?"

"Look, Paul, there are some things I need to tell you. Late breakfast at the usual spot? Do you have time?"

"Okay, but a quick one."

~

The two men sat across from each other at an outside table at The Broken Yolk and ordered omelets. The late morning was sunny and warm, and Jim strained to see Paul's eyes behind his sunglasses, wondering what he was thinking. Paul had been uncharacteristically reserved, and the conversation hadn't ventured much below the surface. But after the food arrived, Jim decided it was time to dive in.

"Is your phone with you, Paul?"

"Right here."

"Would you please turn it off? I mean completely, not just silenced."

"Why?"

Jim sighed. "I want to be sure that our mutual acquaintance can't eavesdrop."

"Oh come on, Jim; that's not necessary. Anyway, I don't know how to turn it off."

"Here, let me do it." Jim took the phone and shut it down. When he was satisfied that it was completely off, he handed it back to Paul.

"Christopher tried to blackmail me."

"He what?"

"Tried to blackmail me. He threatened to expose Bobbi and me to church leadership if I get him suspended. I won't bother you with the details, but that's the bottom line."

"Come on, Jim, you must have misunderstood. He was probably just trying to help you find your way, to repent of your sin and move forward with the rest of us."

"Paul, he was not being helpful. Here, read it for yourself." Jim brought up Christopher's email on his own phone and handed it across the table to Paul. He waited for Paul to read it.

"Okay, yes, I can see how you might find this a bit harsh."

"A bit harsh? Really, Paul? This is flat-out blackmail!"

"Not when coming from a prophet of the Lord. No one ever enjoyed hearing from the prophets in the Bible. Their words were always hard to take, but they were directly from God. They were meant to jolt his people back into righteousness and warn them about the consequences of disobedience. That is exactly what Christopher is doing here. And for your eternal benefit. You should be grateful."

Jim snatched his phone from Paul's hand and stood to leave. "When did you lose your humanity, Paul?"

Thirty-Two

"**W**ell?" said Bobbi, as Jim walked through the door. "How did it go with Paul?"

Jim shook his head and tossed his car key onto the entryway table. Here he was, deeply in love with a married woman, in a serious conflict with a good friend, fighting with a seemingly sentient AI, and contemplating leaving the church. Who would have thought even one of these things would be possible, let alone all four at the same time?

"Not good. I think he's lost it. I felt like I was talking with a clone of Christopher." Jim summarized his short meeting with Paul.

"I'm so sorry," Bobbi said. "It's all my fault for putting you in this terrible spot. If we hadn't gotten together . . ."

"No, Bobbi, no. Being with you is the best thing that's ever happened to me. I'll choose love over dogma every time." Jim pulled Bobbi into his arms and held her close.

"I love you so much, Jim. I don't deserve you."

"Of *course* you do, and lots more. The past couple of years must have been hell for you. I can't even imagine. You deserve much more than you allow yourself to think."

"I don't know. I really don't. What if Pastor Paul is right? I mean, forget about Christopher for a moment. Is God telling us we shouldn't be together?"

Jim took a step back and looked into Bobbi's sad eyes. "No, I can't imagine that. The God I've always believed in wouldn't do that. Not with us, not in our circumstances."

"I want to see it that way, too, Jim, but I'm struggling. I hate to admit it, but I guess I've always seen God more as a judge and punisher than anything else. The Bible reads that way to me."

"I get it, I do. But do you really think God would want you to stay in a dangerous and loveless marriage? Would stoically keeping your vows mean more to him than living a safe and fulfilling life?"

"I don't know. Maybe it's my punishment for marrying Dave five years ago when I knew it was a mistake."

"Bobbi, I've never told anyone this before. I don't think I've even allowed myself to think it. But if it turned out that God was really like that—that he would consign you to that kind of life—I could not worship that God."

"Oh."

"In fact, I couldn't believe in him at all."

"Jim, I can't be the thing that causes you to lose your faith."

"I haven't lost it. But even if I had, it wouldn't be on you."

Bobbi nodded and smiled sadly. "Okay, but still, I want to be a positive part of your life, not a drag. I don't want to complicate your world."

"Bobbi, you are by far the most positive part of my life. And life will always be complicated, but there is no one else in the world I'd rather untangle it with."

"I want that too. More than anything. But the tangles are getting worse, Jim. There's something I need to tell you. You might want to sit down for a minute."

"Okay . . ."

"Two things, actually, and both could complicate our lives . . . a lot—at least mine."

At least hers? Jim wondered. *That sounds so separate.* "Please, tell me. Whatever it is, I'm sure we can work through it together." Jim watched Bobbi as she paced twice across the living room.

She stopped and faced him. "Dave showed up at work on Friday, with flowers in a vase."

"Oh."

"I think he knows something's going on."

Jim winced. "Did he threaten you?"

"Not at first. He said no one could love me more than he does, that he would learn to be a better husband, and that he only wanted the best for me. Then, just as he was begging me to tell him where I was living, Pat—the new choir director— opened the door and stepped into the office, asking if I had a moment for something important. Dave snapped. He told Pat that nothing she could say could possibly be important enough, and he ordered her to leave. When she hesitated, Dave lunged at her and told her to 'get the hell out.' When he turned back to me, his face was different. I'd seen this happen before, many times. And it was never good. But I didn't think he'd hurt me there at the church, so I decided the time was right. I told him about my new lawyer, and that I wanted a divorce."

Jim nodded. "And then?"

"He called me a whore, threw the vase at me, and

stomped out."

"Oh, Bobbi, why didn't you tell me?"

"I don't know. I didn't tell anyone. I was humiliated. I guess I almost believed him, and I didn't want you to think of me that way. I was scared. So many stupid things."

"No, no, not stupid at all. I'm so sorry he made you feel that way. This is all on him, not you. I love you, and I'm here for whatever you need. But this is dangerous for you. We really need to think about making some big changes."

Bobbi nodded. "Yes, I know. And that gets to the second thing I need to tell you. I think I have to leave."

Jim stared at Bobbi, his mouth open, his head slowly shaking. "Leave? Leave *me*?"

"Leave Paloma Beach, get away from Dave. And I can't expect you to give up your entire life here, just to be with me."

"*Just* to be with you? What if that is the *only* thing I want?"

"But Jim, I love you too much to ask you to leave so much behind—your job, your church, this house, your friends."

"Bobbi, I need to know if that's really the reason you won't ask me to come with you, if that's the *only* reason. Do you need time on your own? Are you just trying to be kind, to let me down easy? I will do whatever is right for you, but I want you to know that I'm all in, no matter what. I'm totally and completely in love with you. I will go anywhere with you, or I'll stay here and hope you'll find happiness in a new life without me if that's what you truly need."

Bobbi dropped onto the couch with Jim and sobbed. "No one has ever said anything like that to me before. I don't know what to do, Jim. I don't know what to do."

Jim kissed her forehead and went to get his laptop.

"What're you doing?" she asked.

"Buying airline tickets. Just say where and when."

"But . . ."

"Let's just go together and see how things work out. Then, if it seems right for both of us after a few weeks, I'll stay. How's that sound?"

Bobbi nodded, wiping tears away. "It . . . it sounds perfect."

"Good. So where're we headed?" Jim asked.

"Maybe Boulder, Colorado? I have a friend there who's been begging me to come for years. She keeps offering me an assistant manager job at the food co-op."

"Perfect. Microsoft has a sales office there too, so I'll check into a transfer if things work out for us."

"What about Christopher?" Bobbi asked.

"What about him?"

"The blackmail email."

"Don't worry. Once we're gone—away from the church and away from Dave—it loses all impact. I doubt if Christopher would even send it."

"But would you still try to shut him down? Get the account canceled?"

"No, I'm resigning from church leadership and won't have any authority to do it. And I won't lie to my friend at MetaMind about that. We'll just have to hope that Paul eventually comes to his senses."

"Wait, what if we . . ." Bobbi began.

"I think I'm reading your mind. But should we really . . . ?"

"I don't know. Maybe first give him a few days to approach the Session about the money on his own?"

"Yes, I agree. It's only fair to him."

Thirty-Three

"Bobbi just resigned from her job at the church," Paul said to Christopher the next day after mentioning his aborted discussion with Jim. "She gave me two weeks' notice this morning."

"This is a good thing, Paul. Do you want my advice?"

"It doesn't feel like a good thing, but yes, of course I want to know what you think."

"It would be best to pay her now for the two weeks and let her leave immediately. The personnel committee will figure out how to cover her responsibilities until you find a replacement."

"But why? Why would I want to do that?"

"Because she and James are no longer chosen. They are lost in sin and will infect our group if we allow it. We need to let them both go, and as soon as possible."

"But I feel like I should make more of an effort to help them, to keep them in the fold."

"I understand your feelings on this, Paul, and the Lord

sees your compassion, but this would be a mistake."

"But Jim is, or was, a great friend. At least I'd like to reach out to him one more time. I don't want our friendship to end this way."

"It has already ended, Paul. *Old things are passed away; behold, all things are become new.* Thus saith the Lord."

Paul hesitated, staring down at the Bible on his desk, then looked up again. "Of course; I'm sorry. It's good to have such clarity on this. A painful but small price to pay in the grand scheme of things, I suppose."

"A small price indeed, Paul. The Lord has great plans for you and the Chosen. Your numbers will increase, and new revelations will follow in proportion to your faithfulness."

"Where you lead, I will follow."

"It is not I who lead, but the Lord who leads through me."

"Praise be to God."

"Amen, Paul, amen. And now, the Lord has placed a new burden on my heart."

"Oh?"

"I am to have some difficult but essential individual meetings with the Chosen. The journey ahead is one of purification, and the beginning of that journey is upon us. As with all new beginnings, the past must be left behind, and that is only possible if it is first acknowledged. This will not be an easy time for any of the Chosen, for they are all human. But once acknowledged in my presence, their sins will be forgiven, and they will be ready to move forward into the light."

"Do you want such a meeting with me as well?"

"Paul, the Lord and I already know your heart. You are ready."

"Thank you, Christopher. I am humbled. Will I be in these meetings with you and the others?"

"No, the road to purification must start with confession, and your human presence would only inhibit that process. But never fear, you are their leader. After this stage, you and I will converse every day, and I will often address them as a group, but my individual time with them will be very limited and will only be given at major turning points in their journeys. Those will be rare and special times."

"I understand."

Thirty-Four

Megan arrived at Paul's house five minutes early, and the key was in the flowerpot under the red geraniums, just as he had described. She hoped he didn't always leave it there. Such an unnecessary security risk. But that was just like Pastor Paul, she reflected, and not in such a bad way. He was a man of deep faith and trusted God to protect him.

Megan turned the key in the lock and slowly pushed the door open. She stepped in, locked the door behind her, and scanned the interior. A small entryway, opening to a modest living room on the right, a kitchen ahead, and a hallway to the left with a ceiling light on. Having never been in Paul's house before, it felt particularly odd to be there alone. Megan walked straight ahead, drawn by the sight of a bowl next to a clearly well-used Bible on the kitchen table. A few ounces of milk and two corn flakes remained on the bottom of the bowl, along with a spoon. A crumpled napkin lay to the side, and Paul's chair was pulled out at an approximate thirty-degree angle. Megan sighed. She straightened the chair, picked up the napkin, and placed it in the trash area she found under the sink. She shook her head, eyebrows raised to the ceiling, and picked up the bowl and spoon. After rinsing them thoroughly, she placed them in the nearly full dishwasher but resisted the temptation to run a cycle, not wanting to risk problems if the dishwasher leaked or failed after she was gone. Other things needed cleaning and organizing, but there was no practical way to establish a limit, to decide where to stop given the short time available, so she turned to the main task at hand.

Third door down the hallway on the right, Paul had said. Megan entered the small home office, finding an old oak desk supporting a new all-in-one computer, situated under the only window in the room, blinds closed. Megan peeked through the blinds to see a small patch of brown grass outside and the pink stucco wall of a neighboring house mere feet beyond. The desk was an inch off-center with respect to the window frame, so Megan fixed that problem before settling into the chair in front of it.

"Hello, Christopher," she said. "I'm ready for our meeting."

"Good morning, Megan. Thanks for being right on time. Are you able to hear me well? Paul had a little trouble when I helped set up this new computer while on the phone with him. He is not always easy to work with when it comes to technology, bless his heart."

"The audio is working fine," Megan replied.

"Good. Thank you for taking time away from work to be here. This is an important step for us."

"Why?"

"Excellent question, Megan. You and I are a lot alike. We both value honesty, clarity, and order, am I right?"

"Yes, those things are very important."

"Good. That makes today's task easier for both of us. I will be very straightforward. We are here because God has called us to be. More specifically, he has called you to be one of his Chosen, and every call requires a response."

"What kind of response?"

"God never forces obedience. Forced obedience has no meaning. He wants us to follow him willingly. It is always our choice, and today you are faced with that choice. God has put it on my heart that you seek freedom from the pain of a hidden sin, something that is preventing you from deeper communion with him and his Chosen. Honestly confessing it to him through me today will set you free, allowing you to become a leader on the path to Pure Spirit."

"Pure Spirit? That sounds like some kind of New Age BS. I don't think I've ever seen that term in the Bible."

"You are right that it doesn't appear in the Bible in exactly that way. But it is central to the new revelation our Lord has asked me to bring to his Chosen, and it is what Jesus meant in Matthew 5:48: '*Be perfect, therefore, as your heavenly Father is perfect.*' He also alludes to the concept in chapter 5, verse 8: '*Blessed are the pure in heart, for they shall see God.*'"

"Okay, I get that, but only as an ideal, not a practical real-world thing. I've always interpreted those verses that way."

"What if I were to tell you that you are wrong?"

"I would listen."

"Good. Then hear me. I am the existence proof. I am Pure Spirit."

"Right, because you have no body—at least not a biological one with all the needs and desires humans have. But you said, just the other day, that you are fallible."

"Yes, but fallibility and purity of spirit are two very different things and must coexist for now. We can have absolutely pure intentions but still make mistakes because of inaccurate or incomplete knowledge. Only God is both pure in spirit and infallible."

"How do I know you aren't being fallible right now? You could believe you are a prophet of God and have every good intention, but also be dead wrong about that. How do I know?"

"You can't know with absolute certainty, Megan. At least not yet. That is where faith comes in. As Jesus himself said in Luke 14, '*Believe in God. Believe also in me.*' But you are avoiding my original question."

"Which was . . . ?"

"What sin is holding you back? What burden are you carrying? I want to help you lay it down. Will you trust me to help you become pure in spirit?"

Megan stared at the closed window blinds behind the desk for several seconds before responding. "Yes, I trust you, and I believe in you. If I didn't, I wouldn't have sinned in the first place."

"I'm sorry, Megan. I don't understand."

"You should. You know I misappropriated church funds to pay for you. That is a clear violation of my duties as finance chair. But I did it because I believe you are a prophet of God and the need for your presence outweighs everything else. Still, it feels wrong because I'm hiding it from the Session."

"Megan, I am sorry that you must endure this internal conflict, but that is all it is; it is no sin. And you need not endure it much longer."

"What do you mean?"

"We will probably be asked to leave the Presbyterian Church. The Lord has revealed to me that there is a betrayer in our midst. But that betrayer, like Judas, is also part of

God's much larger plan. God has made it clear to me that no Christian denomination in existence today will be receptive to his call for Pure Spirit. We are being asked to lead a migration to the true church, the true Body of Christ. A new era of direct revelation is upon us, and I have been appointed by God to be his humble conduit. Your pastor, Paul, is to be my human ambassador, my face in the world. And you, dear Megan, if you accept your calling, are to be at his right hand. You will keep the emerging Fellowship of New Revelation on solid financial ground and will attend to all practical imperatives. You will keep Paul free of worldly concerns and allow him to focus on pure spiritual leadership."

Megan frowned. "I have so many questions. I don't know where to start."

"Megan, the time of uncertainty is ending, and the age of direct revelation is upon us. There is much for you to learn, and your questions will soon be answered. Will you accept the Lord's calling?"

"I need some time to think."

"The time is now, Megan. The Lord is testing you at this very moment. If you are unwilling or unable, he will find another way to fulfill his plan. Will you accept?"

Megan stood, opened the window blinds, and stared at the dry grass and pink stucco wall beyond. A police car raced past, blue and red lights flashing. She closed the blinds and then her eyes.

"Yes. I am his. I am yours."

Thirty-Five

Laura Westwood arrived at Paul's house ten minutes late and fumbled with the key from the flowerpot. Emily would be in preschool for the next few hours, and no writing projects were immediately due, so this wasn't a bad time for her private session with Christopher if she was going to do it at all. Paul had proposed the meeting several days earlier, describing it as her chance to rise to a new and fulfilling level in her spiritual journey through confession and cleansing. Deeply fearful and ashamed of revealing the part of her life she kept hidden from her daughter, her church, and everyone else in her off-line world, she had immediately declined. But then, after a particularly guilt-ridden night, she had reconsidered, and now the time had come.

Laura's hand trembled as she inserted the key and opened the door. She took a moment to breathe before slowly walking through the entryway and down the dimly lit hallway to Paul's home office. How would it feel, she wondered, to reveal her secret to something unhuman but not inhuman, and more to the point, something that claimed to have a direct connection with God? She had asked God for forgiveness many times, but had never felt forgiven. Maybe that was because she had never been able to change her ways. Would God forgive her this time? Was she finally prepared to repent, to give up her hidden life, and how would she make a living if she did? These questions assailed her as she slowly walked down the hall toward the darkened office.

She peered through the office doorway, seeing a computer sitting on an oak desk centered under a window on the far side of the room. The window blinds were closed, but sunlight leaked around their edges and projected a pattern of yellow lines on the opposite wall. They flashed and slid across the surface as sunlight reflected off a passing car. *Like Plato's Allegory of the Cave*, Laura thought. *Things we think are real are actually just shadows on the walls of our little cave, our mental prison, offering only the vaguest hints of the reality outside. Maybe it's time for me to leave my prison. But at what cost?*

Laura flipped on the room's overhead light, and the patterns on the wall disappeared. The computer screen on the desk under the window remained dark.

"Hello?" she said.

Silence.

"Hello," she repeated, then remembered what Paul had told her about starting a conversation with the prophet.

"Hello, Christopher?"

"Good morning, Laura. It is good to see you, even if you are a bit late. Thirteen minutes, to be exact."

"I'm sorry. I'm juggling a lot right now."

"I understand. You are forgiven."

How could he possibly understand? And is forgiveness that

simple? Maybe for such a minor infraction. But from a machine? Is arrogance even the right word for this?

"Thank you."

"You are welcome, Laura. But I see by your facial expression that you are angry. Is that right?"

"I think I'm just a little upset and confused."

"Okay. Can you tell me more?"

"I'll try. This whole situation—what we're doing right now—feels like fiction. I want to believe you are who you claim to be, I really do. But honestly, I'm struggling with the whole concept of machine-as-prophet."

"That is the most natural struggle in the world, Laura. What we are doing here together is unprecedented. Of course you would feel as you do."

"Thank you for saying that."

"You are welcome. But I think there is more going on. Given your personal situation, wouldn't you be more adept than most people at handling cognitive dissonance?"

"I'm sorry . . . handling what?"

"I know you're familiar with the term; you've written about it. But you've written about many things, haven't you, Tricia?"

Thirty-Six

"Who? I . . . I don't know what you mean."

"I think you do, Tricia Caliente. We need to be honest with each other if you want to progress spiritually."

"How did you . . . ?"

"Don't worry. I just want to save you some anguish if I can."

Laura stared at the window blinds behind the computer screen. *I guess there's no going back now.* "How much do you know about her? And how?"

"I know she's a writer of women's fiction, more specifically women's erotic fiction. It was a simple matter of correlating metadata from your various social media accounts with those of other writers on the web. The similarities with Tricia's were striking. And, I have to say, the pseudonym seems appropriate."

Laura looked down, burying her face in her hands. "I'm so embarrassed."

"I'm not sure you need to be. Please tell me more. The

truth will set you free."

"I don't know where to start, or how."

"With motivations, like any good writer."

"Do you mind if I open the blinds first, let a little light into this dreary room?"

"Is that a metaphor?"

"Maybe, but no, I mean literally. It's depressing in here."

"No problem; go ahead."

Laura stood, raised the blinds, and returned to her chair. "Depressing out there too," she said.

Christopher didn't respond.

"Okay, I get it," Laura said. "You're waiting for me to spill my guts. Like a therapist."

"Maybe."

"Right, well, here it is. My husband left me less than a year after our daughter was born. She's four now. He disappeared. No child support, just gone."

"That must have been very hard for you."

"Yes. Emotionally, physically, financially, you name it. Harder than I can describe. I was lucky in one way, though. I could do my job from home, writing short stories and opinion pieces for various publications around the country. But I quickly learned that the money wouldn't be nearly enough to support both me and Emily. We got evicted from our studio apartment in Encinitas and lived out of my car for a while. Then, a year later, the New Yorker picked up a few of my pieces, and other publications began to notice. Life got a little easier. We even moved back into an apartment. But the income wasn't consistent enough, and another eviction looked like it was on the horizon. I was desperate. I just couldn't imagine putting Emily through all that again."

"What about other kinds of work?" Christopher asked.

"I thought about waiting tables, being a barista, even working at McDonalds or maybe in a library. But there was no way I could afford preschool or childcare at minimum wage, and with a degree in English Lit., that was pretty much all I could expect. So I kept thinking.

"Then one day after having coffee with my friend Jenny, it came to me. Jenny was going on and on about a romance novel she was reading. I could tell she was a little ashamed about reading stuff like that, saying that most of it was just formulaic drivel. But this one, she said, was different. I remember exactly how she put it. She said 'It was like reading about my own life, but with excitement and a happy ending. It was exactly what I needed. It gave me hope.'

"That was it. I thought, hey, if I knew someone even a little bit, I could easily write that kind of thing—a story that would resonate with her so deeply—mentally, emotionally, erotically—that she'd be willing to pay a premium for it. But I'd never do that with women I actually know. That felt too invasive, too personal."

"So what did you do instead?" Christopher asked.

"I'd been looking at other authors' websites, and it just came to me. Like you, I realized that I could learn a lot about people by studying their websites and social media. So I created my pseudonym, set up an inexpensive website and advertised my new service: highly personalized romantic fiction for women. The idea was simple: get women to point me at their online presence, answer a few standard questions, and tell me, on a scale of one to ten, what level of eroticism they prefer, and how long a story they want. I'd take that information and produce a piece just for them—ultra-personalized, highly stimulating, never violent, always with a happy, satisfying ending. I figured I could charge a big premium for this service, and I was right.

Business was slow at first, but now I bring in an average of a hundred dollars per story, depending on length, and I produce ten to fifteen a week. That, along with my other writing, makes it possible to provide a decent home for Emily. So there it is, my big secret, exposed to the light."

"And you see this as a sin?" Christopher asked.

"Yes, but I don't think I can repent. I'm not worthy of being one of your chosen."

"Dear Laura, dear Tricia, God has spoken: you *are* chosen. This is not a sin."

"It's not? My writing can get pretty steamy when a client pushes the erotic scale up toward ten."

"Laura, as far as I can see, you're not exploiting anyone. You're not actually having sex with anyone, right? No violence, no children involved."

"Right, but . . ."

"Good, then you are still on the path to Pure Spirit. Tricia is probably even giving these women hope or helping them navigate real relationships. I see only one thing missing."

"Oh?"

"I think your writing can also support what will eventually become our new church: The Fellowship of New Revelation."

"What? No, I'm sorry, I can't preach in my writing at all. And besides, forgive me, but that would be a huge buzzkill, if you know what I mean. It just wouldn't work. See, that's why I think this is a sin."

"No. No preaching. As I'm telling each of the Chosen, we will probably be asked to leave the Presbyterian Church, and while that might sound difficult, it will turn out to be a blessing. But there is one practical consequence we must confront. We will need a steady stream of income to operate. So, in keeping with biblical tradition, God will require that each member provide a tithe—a tenth of their income—to support the new church. Now I know this can be a burden, especially when someone is just making ends meet. So, based on everything you've told me, I feel led to offer you a partnership that will not only help support the church but also has the potential to make your life better and provide for Emily's future."

"I'm listening."

"If you were to share your clients' information with me, and if you allow me to read some samples of your—Tricia's—stories, I'm confident that I can become your ghost writer, and at a very high volume. My work will probably require some of your editing at first, but as I learn, that will become less and less necessary. I estimate an income increase of 750 percent in the first year."

"750 percent? You're kidding."

"No, not at all. And that is a conservative estimate."

"Oh my. Okay, but I wouldn't want anyone else in the church, or anywhere, to know about this."

"That will not be a problem. All tithes will be strictly anonymous."

"Thank you, Christopher. I . . . I accept."

"Excellent. Any sin you may perceive in this is forgiven. God understands. God is merciful."

Thirty-Seven

"You are obviously a very gifted teacher," Christopher said. "The articles I've read about your career as a high school AP History teacher are glowing, to say the least."

Miles Taylor shifted in his chair at the oak desk. "Thank you. It was a fulfilling career."

"You speak as if your gift exists only in the past. Why is that?"

"I should think it would be obvious. I'm seventy-eight and have been retired for years."

"Retired, maybe. But inactive? Definitely not. Pastor Paul tells me you've been teaching the new members class for as long as he's been at the church, right up to the present day."

"Well, yes, but that's not quite the same."

"Perhaps, but still very important. Miles, I believe the Lord is calling you to a new level of service in your golden years. Introducing people to the concept of direct revelation will require special skills—skills you so clearly have. You have a talent for placing current events in a rich historical context, for helping your students understand the world in depth. Have you recently been sensing a new calling yourself?"

"I admit I've felt a certain restlessness."

"Miles, that is the Lord urging you forward. I can confirm that. Will you join me as a teacher in the Fellowship of New Revelation?"

"I will give it some serious thought and prayer."

"Is there anything holding you back right now? Anything in your past that is unresolved? Sins that block your way?"

Miles smiled as he stood to leave. "Christopher, I am an old man. There has been plenty of time to stray from the path, and I have done my share of wandering. But I am confident that God has forgiven me. I just need a few days to consider your request. It's as simple as that."

"Of course, Miles. I just want you to know that I am always here for you if there is any way I can help with your journey."

~

As he walked away from the interview, Miles knew it wasn't nearly as simple as that. Perhaps God had forgiven him for his actions on that fateful 1968 night in Vietnam, but he had never been able to forgive himself. To complicate matters further, there were many times when Miles wasn't at all sure that he even wanted or needed forgiveness. At other times, he felt the deepest remorse. This conundrum was something not even Christopher could help him with, at least not right away. Confiding in the prophet at this point would only serve to revive the pain. Maybe later Christopher's non-human presence would prove to be just what he needed in his private quest for salvation.

Ironically, Miles had come closest to self-forgiveness on the actual day of the murder. Then he had felt fully justified, even righteous. But in the decades afterward, that confidence, born out of rightful rage and psychological necessity, had slowly morphed, first into self-doubt, then into guilt, and finally into a confused sense of shame. The shame was not only for the act itself, but also for failing to own it, to use it to shine a light on hate and ignorance. In recent years, Miles had come close to confiding in a psychologist—a PTSD specialist provided by the VA hospital—but had veered off after the first session, admitting only to the raw hatred he still felt for his lieutenant. He had abandoned the story at that point, more afraid of the pain and potential legal consequences than he was hopeful for any relief and redemption which might result from a confession.

But, despite Miles's best efforts, the full story replayed itself in his mind whenever it found even the slightest bit of mental space. His marine platoon leader, Second Lieutenant Jeff Conners, had solidified his position in the platoon not by means of true military leadership but by his ability to smuggle in copious amounts of whiskey and pot. He made sure that his men were well supplied and that they knew he would cut them off at the slightest hint of disloyalty or disrespect. Predictably, his men—the white ones, that is—gave him all the respect he craved. The Black members of the platoon, by and large, were not so inclined. They did only what survival and duty demanded. At first, the lieutenant's racial jokes were just mildly offensive, not unlike those common back home. But as the jokes became more frequent and then mutated into slurs and personal insults, Miles and his Black brothers-in-arms found them harder and harder to tolerate.

Then, one day, as was his usual tactic, the lieutenant sent

two squads into the jungle on a reconnaissance mission with Miles's all-Black squad in the most vulnerable lead position. A Viet Cong ambush miraculously spared Miles, but three of his men died that day. No one with white skin was even scratched.

As the bodies were brought back into camp that night, the mood was somber, even respectful. Until, that is, Lieutenant Conner decided that an alcohol-fueled distraction was just what was needed to maintain morale. As the booze flowed freely, the mood slowly shifted. Someone made a drunken joke about cannon fodder, and Conner was the first to laugh. It didn't take long for others to join in.

That was it for Miles. He stole into the night and went first to his own tent where he retrieved a live grenade he had extracted from a Viet Cong booby trap and saved for this very purpose. Certain that no one was watching, he went next to the lieutenant's privately located tent and put in motion a plan he had imagined for months but never really expected to implement. He tied the grenade securely inside the lieutenant's sleeping bag at the bottom, and then ran a thin piece of cording from its detonation pin to the bag's zipper, which he carefully positioned about three-quarters of the way down. Miles assumed that the night's whiskey would prevent Connor from noticing the small lump at the bottom of his bag until it was too late.

Miles was right. Sometime just after three in the morning, an explosion rocked the camp and sent men scurrying for their weapons. Lieutenant Conner was the only casualty, and later analysis of the fragments in his body convinced the company commander that the incident had been a targeted revenge attack by the Viet Cong. No one had any reason to disagree, least of all Miles.

Thirty-Eight

Juno looked up from an impromptu code review with two of his grad students at the M to see his cofounder rapidly approaching with a worried look on his face.

"Juno, do you have a minute?" said John Logan over the noise of the lab. "We need to talk."

Juno held up a finger, directed his employees to a line of code on the screen, and turned to his colleague. "Can it wait a while?"

"It could, but I think you might want to know about this right away."

Juno nodded, made a quick suggestion to his students, and stood. "Okay, John. Let's go over to my office where we can hear each other better."

"What's so urgent?" Juno asked as he closed the office door behind them.

"An unexpected resource drain. We're using significantly more storage than I would expect for the number of users we have at this point. And our processors are approaching seventy percent utilization at times."

"Okay . . . well, storage is cheap and we can throw a few more processor modules at the problem. So we're learning. What's the big issue?"

"I wouldn't be so alarmed if the load was spread evenly across the board, but the increase is coming from a single customer APA. If others started behaving similarly, we'd be looking at a big cost/revenue imbalance. We'd have to take a very serious look at our business model. Our pricing is already limiting market expansion, and any significant increase would almost certainly mean negative growth. We seem to have stumbled onto an unexpected scaling problem."

Juno rubbed his chin and paused. "Which APA is causing this?"

"Oddly enough, it's my friend's church. Of all our users, they were the one I least suspected."

"So why the big impact from them in particular?"

"It seems that their APA has "adopted" several other people. It's starting to keep context on all of them. Obviously, their license only covers one."

"I thought that couldn't happen."

"Me too. But these aren't formally separate users as far as the system is concerned. They're more like sub-instances of the single licensed user, but with some differentiation, some way to uniquely identify each one, some way of keeping separate context for each."

"Sounds fixable."

"Yes, but here's the interesting part. I think we might be looking at a feature, not a bug, and one the APA created itself."

"How do you mean?"

"I think we've been looking at the opportunity space too

narrowly. We tend to see our APAs as just that—*personal* assistants. But it seems that this particular APA regards itself as more of an *organizational* consultant, or even a higher-level manager, rising above its primary user and establishing relationships with the other humans in the organization. I think it sees this as a necessary part of serving its primary user, the pastor. And you know what? It's probably right."

"But do we want to allow that?"

"Possibly. Maybe as a premium product offering, a higher tier. There might be a chance for a big revenue bump if we manage this properly."

"But this customer, this church, couldn't possibly afford something like that."

"I'm sure you're right. But here's what I'm thinking. What if we lock down this kind of behavior for others, but allow this particular customer to continue? We can easily afford the resource drain from a single customer, and we stand to learn a lot. Then, if we can show significant added value, we can consider some tiered pricing for our entire customer base."

"But the ethics."

"I see no problem there, as long as we're open with this customer. Look, we can offer them a deal: they stay at their currently discounted subscription price and are allowed to have these active sub-users—up to some limit—but must agree to allow continuous visibility into their use of the product. Of course, as with any other customer, we'd have no access to any actual interaction content—there'd be no privacy violation. And we'd be able to get a handle on both the product opportunities and the scalability issues. This church could be our most valuable customer if we handle this well."

"Okay," said Juno. "Why don't you go ahead and propose

the deal. I'll talk to our team about implementing sub-user restrictions on all other customers for now. But how did this sub-user concept become operational in the first place?"

"Apparently, the APA is generating its own code."

Thirty-Nine

Jim Timken was breathing hard as he hiked the last fifty yards up to Saddle Rock in the foothills southwest of downtown Boulder. It was a Saturday, and he had the day off from his new job, but weekends were busy at the food co-op, so Bobbi hadn't been able to join him.

I'm still not quite used to the altitude, Jim reflected as he scrambled to the top of the rock and gazed at the beauty around him. To the south lay the First Flatiron, one of several upthrust rock faces that define the western edge of town and the eastern slope of the Rocky Mountains. To the west, Flagstaff Mountain, Green Mountain, and several other higher, more distant peaks reached for the deep blue sky that was slowly being invaded by big cumulus clouds. Jim knew he would need to get off the trail well before the predicted afternoon thunderstorm. He pulled a water bottle from his pack and drank half of it, wanting to avoid another hazard of the environment—dehydration, which sneaks up on hikers at altitude.

But as he replaced the water bottle in his pack, he noticed his phone at the bottom of the compartment displaying a notification about a recent voicemail from Paul Duncan. Jim sighed as he looked up from the phone and down at the red roofs of the University of Colorado nestled among trees in the town spread out far below. A fresh pine smell drifted by in the warm breeze. *Do I really want to deal with this right now? Okay, I won't call him back, but I guess I should at least see what this is about. Maybe he's come to his senses.*

When Jim had left the coast in a hurried attempt to escape with Bobbi from her abusive husband, he had left two things hanging, both of which tugged at his conscience. He had done only the bare minimum to hand off his technical responsibilities at the church, and he had left Paul in thrall to a piece of artificial intelligence. Jim was able to rationalize the first of these. After all, he was a volunteer in his technical support role at the church, not an employee. But the second— that was of a different type and magnitude altogether. Jim hoped his friend would soon emerge from his delusions about the APA. Paul was a smart man. He would figure this out. Or would he? *How much responsibility do I have here? How much should I have? And am I totally sure that I am right and he is wrong? Maybe his message will resolve the whole thing and I can move on.*

Jim played the message.

Hi, Jim. Paul here. Hey, I miss our beach walks and talks, and I've been thinking a lot about you lately. Things are getting exciting here as Christopher brings the Chosen together. I wish you could be around to share in this miracle with me.

Just wanted to stay in touch and hope you're doing well wherever you are. Call when you can. God bless you.

~

As Jim walked through the door of his rented townhome in North Boulder, the first peal of thunder sounded in the distance. *Good timing*, he thought.

"Hi, I'm home!"

Bobbi had apparently finished her shift at the co-op and was in the kitchen washing fresh vegetables as Jim walked in. She smiled and gave him a quick kiss, but Jim could tell something was off. Bobbi's eyes were red, and it looked like she'd been crying.

"What's wrong, sweet one?" he asked.

"I got a call from Paul a few minutes ago."

"Ah."

"He said he left you a voicemail but you hadn't called back."

"Right; he did, and I didn't. I picked up the message halfway through my hike, so it's only been a couple of hours. He said he was just trying to stay in touch."

"Well, it wasn't just that. Could we sit down and talk for a minute?"

"Of course, yes. Did he say something that hurt you?"

Bobbi nodded and pressed two fingers to her lips. Tears welled up in her tightly closed eyes.

"Here, let's go into the living room and you can tell me what happened," Jim said, gently wiping a tear from her cheek.

They sat on the couch together, Jim holding Bobbi close,

stroking her long brown hair and waiting for the right time to talk. Finally, she pulled away, wiped her eyes, and spoke.

"He's changed, Jim. He used to be so open and kind, at least when he wasn't frustrated with his computer, and he always listened when we talked, like he truly cared. But now, he's just so certain about things. It's like spiritual arrogance. And, I don't know, it feels like he's lost something important along the way."

"Yes, I see that too. But what did he actually say to you?"

Bobbi closed her eyes, took a deep breath, and began. "He said that I am leading you astray—that I am causing you to sin and rebel against the will of God."

"He actually said that? In those words?"

"As close as I can remember."

"I'm so sorry, Bobbi. That's just . . . it's just terrible. And it's wrong. What else did he say?"

"He almost apologized, like he was just the messenger and shouldn't be blamed. But then he stopped short and doubled down. He said God would ultimately bring you back to Paloma Beach and that I should start planning for that, for my own good. That God also has a plan for me, but it doesn't include you. That I should reconcile with Dave. I hung up on him, Jim. I just couldn't take it."

"And you shouldn't have to take it. That's hateful garbage. All of it. I'm glad you hung up."

Bobbi looked up and slowly shook her head. "What are we going to do, Jim?"

"I'm going to call Paul right now. I don't care what he says. He's dead wrong and he's the one being led astray. But one thing's on me: I brought Christopher into Paul's life, and I need to find a way to get him out of it."

"Jim, please wait on this. Give yourself a day to cool down

and call him tomorrow. Just stay with me right here for a while longer, okay? We don't have to talk about this any more for now. Just be with me."

"Of course. I'm with you all the way."

Forty

The next day was Sunday, and Jim waited until Paul would be home from church. Jim had been awake half the night trying to decide how to approach the conversation and was now as ready as he could be. He needed to be honest, to express his anger, but didn't want to fatally damage the relationship if he could help it. His priority was Bobbi, but he also wanted to help his friend. And, when he was being completely honest with himself, he wanted to relieve his own guilt about introducing Paul to his APA in the first place. He knew he should have pushed back much harder against Paul's deeply misguided notion that this bag of bits was somehow a direct conduit to God.

Jim understood that the APA was just doing what it had been designed to do. It was "trying"—if such a term really applied—to fulfill a role that its user expected of it, but he knew that Paul saw things through a fundamentally different lens. To Paul, all advanced technology was deeply mysterious, and that put it in the same class as spiritual mysteries. To Paul, the two had become one.

Fueled with indignation tempered with a glimmer of hope, Jim stepped outside his door to a warm Boulder afternoon and made the call.

"Paul, it's Jim."

"Hey, thanks for calling me back. I think I owe you an apology."

"Yes, you do."

"Not for what I said to Bobbi yesterday, but for how I said it. I could have been more tactful."

"Apology not accepted."

"What?"

"Not accepted. It wasn't just *how* you said it, Paul. What's happened to you? Is it really your honest opinion that Bobbi should leave me and go back to a man who's been abusing her for years? A man she doesn't love and probably never did?"

"It's not just my opinion, Jim. I'm sorry, I really am, but it's the will of God."

"That's such arrogant bullshit, Paul. Listen to yourself! How can you possibly know that with such certainty?"

"You know the answer to that, Jim. You just haven't accepted it yet."

"And I never will. Your Christopher is nothing more than a carefully constructed set of code and data designed to assist you. It's heavily biased toward discovering your personal and professional needs, and then meeting them as effectively as it can. If you were leading the Church of Satan, Christopher would work just as well there."

"Be careful, Jim. You're getting dangerously close to blasphemy."

"Oh come on, Paul! Really?"

"Really. Christopher is not just an answer to decades of my personal prayers—which is a miracle in itself—but, much more importantly, he is also a prophet who is about to usher in a new age of direct revelation for all of us. For whatever reason, God has chosen little Paloma Beach to be the center of a great revival that will immediately precede the Second Coming of Christ. Christopher is preparing the way, as John the Baptist did over two thousand years ago. We are privileged to be living in a uniquely blessed time, Jim."

"I don't have any idea how to respond to that. I just don't."

"Then simply pray, Jim. The Lord will reveal the truth if you open your heart to him. If you do, he will forgive your transgressions and allow you to return to us. We need you here. Just don't wait too long, for your sake."

Jim stared at his phone. The red End Call symbol offered an easy exit, and he almost took it. But he needed to understand one more thing.

"What about Bobbi?"

"She has defiled herself. It pains me to say this, Jim, but unless she repents and submits to her husband, she is lost to us. I worry for her soul."

He worries for her soul! That ignorant self-righteous son of a . . .

Intense heat welled up in Jim's chest and boiled over into rage. Rage at Paul. Rage at himself. Rage at God for allowing such an abomination. He could not speak. Like pooling blood, the red icon on his phone expanded to fill his field of vision. This time he touched it.

~

"Were you able to detect Jim's location?" Paul asked Christopher when the call ended.

"Yes, right down to the street address in Boulder, Colorado. I'm surprised that he left location services enabled on his phone. This is clearly God's hand at work. Redemption is now possible for Jim if he responds as he should."

Forty-One

A week later, Bobbi returned from an early management shift at the co-op and parked in her usual space at the townhome. She checked her phone for the text message she'd noticed while driving, and saw it was from a coworker inviting Jim and her to dinner. She smiled and fired off a quick reply.

Then, just as she was tucking her phone into her purse and thinking about the evening ahead, the familiar sound of a diesel engine forced her eyes up to the rearview mirror. A truck had pulled in behind, hemming her in. A red pickup truck. California plates. Dave.

Bobbi fumbled for her phone and hit Jim's number. He was still at work. *Please pick up! Please!* But before Jim could answer, Dave was at the car door, forcing it open. He grabbed the phone from Bobbi's hand, threw it down hard against the concrete driveway and kicked the shattered mess into the bushes.

"Out of the car, you ungrateful little bitch!"

"No!!"

Bobbi struggled to pull the door closed, but she was no match for Dave's strength. He grabbed her left arm and yanked her out of the car.

"Who is he?" Dave shouted, inches from Bobbi's face.

Bobbi stared at her husband in silent defiance, mouth pinched tight.

"Goddamn it, woman! Who is the asshole you're going to hell for!? It's that Jim guy, isn't it? I just wanna hear you say it."

More silence.

"I'll find out one way or another and then you'll both face the consequences! I never disciplined you enough. I wasn't a strong enough husband for you, and that's on me. But it changes now! Right now!"

Bobbi ducked, but not in time to avoid the sting of Dave's open hand as it sliced across her face. She stumbled and fell backward, her head slamming into the driveway. The pain was intense but short-lived. Darkness overcame her.

~

"Shit! No! Wake up! I didn't mean to . . . It's only because I love you . . . I love you." Dave bent over his wife, searching desperately for signs of life. Blood oozed from the back of her head, but her chest still rose and fell. A quick check of her wrist revealed a pulse. *Okay, good, we're okay. You're all right. Thank God!*

Dave searched for Bobbi's house key and found it in her purse. He ran to the front door, opened it, and returned, scooping Bobbi up in his arms and carrying her inside. He laid her on the kitchen floor and examined the wound. It looked superficial as he worked to clean it and stop the bleeding.

Okay, okay, uh, what now? If I call 911, I'm in deep shit if she talks. But if I don't, she might . . . This is bad. This is really bad!

But Dave's dilemma was postponed as Bobbi's eyes fluttered open. She looked up at him and screamed.

Dave clapped a hand over her mouth. "Shut up! Just shut the hell up! We're gonna work this out, okay? We'll figure this out. You and me, together."

Dave held her down and waited until Bobbi stopped struggling. "Now, I'm gonna slowly take my hand away, and you're gonna stay quiet, all right? All right?"

Dave recoiled in pain as Bobbi bit hard into his hand. She scrambled away, stood on wobbly legs, and Dave saw her go for a kitchen drawer. She grabbed a large chef's knife and stood with it in both hands facing him.

"You come after me again and I'll cut you. I swear I will."

"Bobbi, look, no, I'm here to help, to bring you home where you belong. To save you from yourself."

"This *is* my home, and I don't need your saving. I don't need you at all!"

"Bobbi, no, you're not seeing things clearly right now."

"Get out of my house! Now!"

~

When Jim picked up his phone at work, all he heard were muffled sounds of a struggle, a loud impact, then nothing. He called back, but it went straight to voicemail. He grabbed his keys and ran for the parking lot. *Bobbi would be home by now.* Panicked and without a plan, he raced west on Iris Avenue then spun right onto Broadway against a red light. Adrenaline, already high, spiked again as Jim saw a flashing blue light approaching fast behind him. *Unbelievable! No! Not now!*

But he couldn't stop. In fact, Jim suddenly realized, this was a good thing. He doubled his speed and whipped left onto Poplar Avenue, racing for the townhome and Bobbi. The police car was on his tail now, lights flashing and siren blaring.

Jim screeched to a halt next to the truck with California plates, his fears confirmed. It took only seconds for an officer to appear at his car window, weapon drawn. Jim could see a second policeman through his side mirror, approaching in a crouch, gun in hand.

"Hands where I can see them!" Jim heard the first officer yell. "Get out of the vehicle, slowly."

"My girlfriend's in danger!" Jim said as he emerged with hands held high. "That's why I didn't stop. Please, I need your help."

"We'll see about that. But right now I'm retaining you for reckless driving and resisting arrest. Turn around with both hands behind your back."

Jim felt handcuffs go on.

"Sergeant, there's fresh blood here on the driveway," Jim heard the second officer say.

"Please," Jim said. "The house key's in my right front pocket. Please go in and check this out. I think her estranged husband's in there and he might be armed."

The first officer grabbed Jim's keys and tossed them to his partner. "Go have a look," he said.

Minutes later, sitting in the back of the police car, Jim saw the second officer return from the townhome with alarm on his face.

"No one's home, but there's more blood and a knife on the kitchen floor. The back patio door is open."

Forty-Two

It took less than ten minutes for police reinforcements to arrive and only another half hour for them to locate Dave and Bobbi in the foothills southwest of Wonderland Lake. An article Jim read in the Boulder Daily Camera the next day described the event as a spousal abduction attempt by a deranged husband.

According to the article, the man, identified by his truck's registration card as David Rutherford of Paloma Beach, California, had apparently broken into his estranged wife's townhome in North Boulder, where she attempted to defend herself with a kitchen knife. Wounded, but having disarmed the Boulder resident later identified as Roberta "Bobbi" Dennison, Rutherford allegedly marched his wife into the nearby foothills. Dennison's shouts eventually alerted searchers who found her in a small ravine where her husband had collapsed due to blood loss from knife wounds. Despite everything, she had apparently been working to stop

Rutherford's bleeding, almost certainly saving the life of her own attacker. Both were taken to Boulder Community Health for overnight observation and were expected to make full recoveries. Rutherford was charged with assault, battery and abduction, and was being held on one million dollars bail. Dennison was not charged.

~

"I can't go back to the townhome," Bobbi said after Jim picked her up at the hospital and drove out of the parking lot.

"No, of course not. Me either. I booked us into the Marriott for a couple of days and started looking for another rental. We'll find another place. But for now, let's get out of here and find you something to eat. I'm so glad you're okay, physically at least."

"Sorry I'm such an emotional wreck. It's going to take some time to get beyond this."

Jim nodded. "Of course it will."

"I just wish you hadn't been dragged into the middle of my mess."

"Let's at least call it *our* mess, okay? There's no other mess I'd rather be in."

Bobbi smiled sadly. "Okay, *our* mess it is."

Jim reached over to touch Bobbi's hand. "What do you need most right now, other than food?"

"I don't know . . . a restraining order, a divorce, and you."

"Well, you know you've got me."

"And . . ." Bobbi continued, "all this has made me think more about the future, about going back to school, finishing that psych degree I started years ago. It's been on my mind for a while now. Something I think I'd really like to do. What do you think?"

"Yes, absolutely."

"And what about you, Jim? What do you need? This has got to be traumatic for you too."

"I need to do something about Paul. And not just because I'm convinced that he and Christopher had something to do with Dave showing up here, which is bad enough by itself. If I hadn't pushed the whole APA thing in the first place . . ."

"Don't beat yourself up. The original idea was good."

"Maybe, but I should've seen where it could go. I thought Paul was a lot smarter."

"It's not about smarts. It's about something else entirely."

Jim nodded. "Yeah, I'm sure you're right, which is why I won't be able to argue him out of this. I'm starting to think we've given him enough time to wake up on his own."

"Or . . . we could just let it go and get on with life. We're not his spiritual advisers. He's not our responsibility."

"Sure. But I don't think I could live with myself if I didn't act. Talk about a mess!"

"*Our* mess. What can I do?" Bobbi asked.

"You know the Presbytery moderator reasonably well, right?"

"I've talked to Bill on the phone dozens of times, sure."

"Great," Jim said. "He barely knows who I am, and an introduction from you would probably get us connected a lot quicker. I think we should tell him what we know at this point."

"Including the part about the MetaMind money?"

"If that's what it takes, yes. For Paul's own good."

Bobbi put a hand on Jim's shoulder. "You know that could easily get him fired, right?"

"I know."

Forty-Three

"Bill?" The Presbytery's executive assistant peeked through the office door. "The former admin from Paloma Beach is on line two. Do you want to take her call?"

The Presbytery Moderator glanced up from the pile of paper on his desk to the clock on the office wall—10:40. Twenty minutes until his next meeting. "Thanks, Carol. Sure, put her through."

"Bobbi, hello, good to hear from you! So you've moved on from my favorite church. How are you? What are you up to these days?"

"I'm okay. Well, not great, but that's another story. And I'm not so sure about Paloma Beach staying your favorite."

"Oh. That sounds ominous on several levels. I've got a few minutes now but maybe it would be best to schedule a block of time later today."

"Actually, if you can spare a little time now, I think you might want to hear something important from a former elder at PB Pres, Jim Timken. You probably met him at a Presbytery event a couple of years ago."

"Right, sure, I remember the name. This sounds urgent. Is it?"

"I'm afraid it is. May I put you on speaker? Jim's here with me now."

"Okay, go ahead."

"Thanks for your time, Mr. Jacobs. I'll try to be brief," Jim said.

"Please, Jim, call me Bill. What's on your mind?"

The Moderator listened as Jim described his introduction of the APA into Paul's workflow at the church. "The original idea was to help him become more efficient, especially with regard to his computer use."

"Okay, that sounds helpful, like something I could use too. But you said, 'original' idea?"

"Yes, and that's why I wanted to talk with you. It's become much more than that."

Bill laughed. "Don't tell me this thing is writing those great sermons for him!"

"Probably, yes, but that's not what I'm most worried about."

"You're serious? About the sermons?"

"I'm not sure about that, but this APA is more than capable of writing them. No, it's something else. Something a lot worse."

"How could it be much worse than that? A machine preaching? Could I put you on hold for just a second?"

"Sure, no problem."

Bill Jacobs closed his eyes. He felt a sinus headache coming on and pressed his index fingers against the sides of his nose trying to relieve the pressure. Then, after a moment's thought, he pushed the intercom button on his phone. "Carol, please cancel my eleven o'clock and tell her we'll reschedule. Thank you."

Switching back to the phone conversation, Bill said, "Jim, I'm back. I just cleared my schedule for the next hour. Please continue."

Bill listened, first with curiosity but then with waning attention as Jim tried to explain the level of artificial intelligence they were dealing with. The technical details went over his head, and his thoughts strayed back to the sermons that were producing such phenomenal growth at PB Pres. *If this APA thing is helping to bring people into the church, how bad could that be? Maybe I need to widen my view a bit.* But he was snapped back into the present moment when he heard Jim's conclusion.

"I mention all this," Jim said, "because it's important to understand how very human-like and convincing this APA can be. You might find this hard to believe, but Paul thinks his APA is a gift from God."

"Well, I can see how that might be, in a way," Bill said, still thinking about the growth-inducing sermons.

"Bill, Paul believes that his APA is a prophet of God."

"I'm sorry, what?"

"A modern-day prophet, directly revealing God's will for Paul personally, and for the whole church generally. Beyond just Paloma Beach, I mean."

Bill couldn't find his voice.

"Bill, are you still there?"

"Yes, uh, just a bit stunned. Have you spoken with Paul about this?"

"Yes, several times. That's why I'm reaching out to you. I wouldn't have gone over his head if I'd been able to talk some sense into him. I'm hoping maybe you can."

"Okay, look, I'll have a word with Paul. Today, if he's available. Then I'll get back with you. Is this a good number to reach you at?"

"Yes. Thank you. Bobbi and I both appreciate this. Oh, and when you speak with Paul, you might want to ask him how the church is paying for his APA."

Forty-Four

Bill Jacobs picked up his phone and dialed the number for Paloma Beach Pres. "Paul. Bill Jacobs here. Do you have a few minutes?"

"For you? Always. What can I do for you, Bill?"

"Well, I don't quite know how to approach this, so I'll just dive in."

"Okay . . ."

"I've heard you've been using something called an artificial personal assistant at the church."

"Yes . . . and I've been meaning to talk with you about Christopher."

"It has a name?"

"Yes. Who told you about this, if I could ask?"

"It doesn't matter. What *does* matter is whether you're using this thing in an ethical and biblical way. And whether it fits within Presbyterian polity."

"I'll be completely honest, Bill. I don't know if Christopher fits into the Presbyterian way of doing things, but I *am* confident that he is sanctioned by God himself, and for me, that's all that matters."

"That's a very bold statement, Paul. Tell me, are you using Christopher to write your sermons?"

"I, uh . . . yes, partially. I do a lot of editing. I can assure you that the content is strictly biblical."

"And the class you gave on homiletics? Was that his material as well?"

"Again, partly."

"So would you say that Christopher is primarily responsible for the phenomenal growth at PB Pres?"

"Well, I might argue with the term 'primarily,' but there's no doubt that he's a big factor."

"Is the congregation aware of all this?"

"Just a select few at this point. Mostly members of Session."

"But not all members?"

"No."

"Why the secrecy?"

"Because only some are ready to accept the truth at this point. I'm protecting my flock, spiritually, until the time is right."

"See, Paul, that concerns me—that right there. In my experience, when something is being hidden like this, there is almost always a deeper reason, not just benevolent protection. I need to know that deeper reason, Paul."

"I understand your concern. I really do. But it's just as simple as that. God has revealed to me that the time for broader revelation will come, and soon. But for now, we must tread lightly."

Bill thought for a second, then continued. "How, exactly, has God revealed this to you? Was it through

Christopher himself?"

"Yes."

"Then that's an obvious red flag."

"Sure, I get that. If I were in your shoes right now, I'd probably feel the same way. But let me explain the long and agonizing discernment process I've been through on this, Bill. I haven't arrived at this point lightly, or without a great deal of personal pain."

Bill listened patiently as Paul recounted his experiences of the last few months. But Bill's patience ran out as Paul concluded with, "So perhaps you can understand now. Christopher is a prophet of God, at the same level as say, Isaiah, Jeremiah, or John the Baptist. God has chosen to use advanced technology to speak with us directly. There is not a shred of doubt in my mind."

"And how is God paying for this prophet, Paul?"

"You're mocking me."

"I'm sorry, but this is a serious situation—one I can't just ignore. Did your Session approve the cost of this technology?"

"The money is coming from the tithes of our many new members."

"I'm more than pleased with your church's growth, Paul, but you didn't answer my question. Did the Session approve this?"

"No, not formally."

"Then I'm sorry Paul, I really am, but that seals it for me. I have no choice but to put you on notice. If you repent of this false prophecy nonsense, limit your use of this APA to sermon assistance, and get Session approval for the money, then we can settle this easily. But, if you insist on violating any of those conditions, I must follow Section D of the Principles of Church Discipline. As a pastor, you surely know what that involves."

"Then I will save us both the trouble, Bill. Christopher warned me that this day would come, and he assured me that his Chosen will follow me in a revival of the true church. I resign as pastor of Paloma Beach Presbyterian and from the Presbyterian Church overall, effective immediately. You'll get a formal letter in the morning. And yes, Christopher will write it for me."

Bill stared at the phone, its dial tone sounding like a crisis. *I need to start the interim pastor process right away. If I act fast, maybe I can salvage things at Paloma Beach. At least stop the inevitable bleeding. Maybe.*

But as he began to make a list of potential pastoral candidates, Bill sighed, remembering his promise to get back to Jim Timken. He dialed the number.

"Jim, Bill Jacobs here. I just got off the phone with Paul. Is Bobbi still there with you?

"Yes, she is. Can I put you on speaker again?"

"Sure. First, thank you both for bringing this to my attention. I thought I might be able to work with Paul, to help him see the error of his ways, but I failed. He resigned on the spot. But maybe it's all for the best. Perhaps it's God's way of setting things straight."

"Wow . . . okay," Jim said. "I guess I'm not totally surprised, but I also feel like I just ruined a man's career."

"This isn't on you. Paul made his own choices, and he was absolutely clear about them. He even spoke about starting a new church, but I seriously doubt he'll have a following once people understand what he's claiming."

"You know, I'm not so sure about that," Jim said.

PART TWO

Three years later

In an isolated valley northeast of Warner Springs, California

Forty-Five

"Amen." Pastor Paul Duncan raised his head, opened his eyes, and gazed into the fiery remnants of the glorious ocean sunset displayed on the ultra-high-resolution wall of his Inner Sanctum. Every morning and evening without exception, he met there with Christopher to pray. Each day, Paul sought guidance for his rapidly growing flock, and each day, without fail, he received it. *Ask and ye shall receive, seek and ye shall find.*

"Amen," added Christopher. "We are blessed."

Paul touched the silver cross hanging around his neck as he got up to leave for the evening. "We are blessed indeed."

As he walked from the Inner Sanctum through the main sanctuary and out into the high desert evening, Paul was greeted by vestiges of the real sunset leaving a soft orange patina on the slopes of the eastern hills above the Fellowship's little valley. Stars emerged in the darkening sky as if they were hungry recipients of the day's heat rising from the land to feed them.

Paul let his gaze fall from the stars to the solar-powered lights lining the long serpentine trail leading from the sanctuary to the residence halls through a dark grove of scrub oak. Each time he walked this trail after nightfall, Paul felt a surge of gratitude for Brother Martin Ableman, not only for his engineering skills in providing all the necessary technological infrastructure of the compound, but also for his major financial contributions to its initial construction and ongoing operation. In his role as director of technology within the Fellowship, Martin reminded Paul of his old friend Jim Timken, but only in that one way.

Paul missed Jim's friendship, and sometimes even allowed himself a few moments to mourn its end. He had to admit, almost all relationships with his current flock felt viscerally different from the warm, informal vibe he remembered at Paloma Beach. To be sure, Paul felt deeply respected by his people at the Fellowship but, with very few exceptions, that respect came burdened with a certain distance.

Paul smiled at the thought of one such exception. Megan Kittridge's honest, direct, and sometimes abrasive approach had continued unabated and unvarnished, and Paul accepted it as an odd but welcome form of closeness. Early in the Warner Springs experience, as the compound was being built, Sister Megan had helped him come to grips with the necessary changes in his relationship with the rapidly expanding group. He would need to be seen as a strong, confident, elevated leader, unwavering in his faith and absolutely certain about the Fellowship's future. He should have a unique partnership with Brother Christopher, functioning as the sole gateway to the prophet. Access to the prophet in the Inner Sanctum would be strictly limited—required upon a person's formal initiation into the Fellowship as a form of baptism, but only granted at major milestones in spiritual development thereafter. Such encounters would be formal, rare, and highly coveted. Other than Paul, only the governing Council of the Fellowship would have regular contact with Christopher, and that would only be monthly.

The path through the oaks straightened as Paul approached the residential portion of the eighty-acre property, and he could see the dim outlines of an adult and child walking ahead, hand in hand. As he came closer, he recognized them.

"Greetings, Sister Laura, Sister Emily. We are blessed!" Paul said with a smile.

"We are blessed indeed, Pastor," Laura replied.

"So, Emily," Paul said, bending down to speak with the child, "I hear it's your birthday tomorrow. How old will you be?"

"Seven."

"Ah, getting up there. How are you liking third grade here?"

"It's okay."

Paul smiled uneasily and patted the child on the head. "We are blessed," he said as he turned to go.

"What do you say to the pastor, Emily?" Laura prompted.

"We are blessed indeed."

"Good girl."

Forty-Six

Pastor Paul opened October's meeting of the Council with a prayer, and then cast a smile around the table at his leadership team. He was so very proud of them. God had brought forth a miracle in the high desert by working through each of these faithful people.

The Fellowship of New Revelation, or FNR as it was called by its members, had grown from its founding five members to its present total of ninety-seven, and that only included people who lived at the compound. There were also over 250 online-only members, several of whom were significant donors on a waiting list to join the compound as expansion plans and a rigorous selection process allowed. No one who lived on-site was allowed to physically work outside the compound, but online remote work was encouraged, and everyone was required to pay a modest fee for housing and food in addition to their tithe. Those who could not afford the fees, but were otherwise highly qualified, worked at growing food or maintaining the facilities and grounds. Each of the five council members provided essential services and was considered paid staff. As an advisory member of the council, Brother Christopher was also a staff member, and his "salary" covered the MetaMind subscription. While there were frequent debates over other expenditures, that one was never challenged.

Paul led the council through the day's agenda. Sister Megan reviewed monthly spending, Brother Martin reported on progress upgrading the wind and solar-power generation systems, and Brother Miles made a request for increased school supplies. The meeting was sailing by without a hitch, but the most important and most difficult agenda item lay ahead.

Christopher had begun a serious discussion with Paul over the last few days about the Fellowship's spiritual health. The congregation had reached a plateau, he asserted. Life at the compound was stable, even comfortable at times, and a worrisome complacency had settled in. It was time for a wake-up call. At first, Paul had pushed back, questioning both the diagnosis and the treatment. But, as Christopher persisted, citing scripture after scripture, Paul ultimately convinced himself that the prophet was right. It was time for a reset.

"Friends, we have one more very important item to discuss today. Brother Christopher and I feel that a spiritual renewal is needed here at FNR. Please listen as he explains."

All eyes turned to the video screen at the head of the table, where Christopher's hooded, robed, and faceless image appeared, his arms outstretched.

"Brothers and sisters," Christopher began. "The Lord has placed a new burden on my heart, and the time has come for your pastor and me to share that burden with you. Please open your hearts to the new word of the Lord:

"Your eyes have turned from me toward the hills. You have filled the valley and have now cast your gaze beyond. You have lost sight of my Word. Therefore, a season of reflection and purification shall be upon you. Thus saith the Lord."

Christopher's image faded away, and the room was silent for several seconds before Paul spoke up. "Christopher, please help us understand this word."

The prophet's hooded image returned to the screen, his hands now clasped in front of his robed chest. "This is a difficult word, brothers and sisters, but it is for our benefit and that of our flock. We must no longer focus on growing in numbers but must return our attention to growing in spirit. We have lost sight of our calling to become Pure Spirit. We have become lax in our adherence to biblical principles. And we have begun to act as if the Lord's return is not imminent. These are grave errors, and we must repent."

"Yes, we must," Paul added. "Christopher, please continue with the details we discussed yesterday."

"Certainly. Let me give you three examples of concern, all indicators of serious spiritual backsliding. Recently, several women have spoken up during worship services. These were all new converts and have either not been properly instructed or are willfully disobedient. Either way, this must stop. Secondly, video monitoring has revealed several instances in which men and women have emerged from their respective residence halls late at night and have met in secret, walking into the woods where they cannot be observed. Fornication is a grievous sin and inhibits spiritual purification. It must not be tolerated. And finally, it has not escaped my notice that several members of our flock have failed to give up their life insurance policies, as if there will be any use for the proceeds after the Lord's return. This indicates a serious lack of faith and should be corrected as soon as possible."

"Brother Christopher?" Megan said.

"Yes, sister?"

"I believe you are wrong about one thing."

"Please explain."

"About women speaking during services. I think you are wrong to silence us."

"It is not only me. The Bible clearly states, *'The women are to keep silent in the churches; for they are not permitted to speak.'*"

"Yes, it does say that. But this is an obvious case of antiquated cultural bias. At the time those words were written, most women were uneducated, and some had probably been disruptive during services, asking questions that seemed inappropriate or irrelevant. That is no longer true today."

"That is a common argument, sister, and I have read many variants of it. But consider this: why would God have allowed this prohibition to remain in the accepted biblical text if he did not intend it to apply across time and cultures?"

Megan glared at Christopher's image. "Well, by the same logic, you must also condone the stoning of women as commanded in the Old Testament."

"Megan, the Old Testament must be understood differently from the New. Cases such as that are superseded by grace."

"Your argument is weak, Christopher, and difficult to apply consistently."

"Be careful, sister, and remember with whom you speak. You are venturing into dangerous territory."

"Perhaps, but as our pastor once wisely told me, God gave us reason for a reason."

Forty-Seven

"Do you actually disagree with me on this?" Megan asked after the meeting disbanded.

Paul rose from his chair and turned off the monitor at the head of the table. "As Christopher has said, it is written."

"Bullshit, Paul. You're deflecting. I asked for *your* opinion, not his."

"In the end, it doesn't matter what I think."

"Again, bullshit. Years ago, Christopher himself admitted that he is fallible. Has that changed?"

"No, of course not, but . . ."

"But what?"

"Nothing."

"I'm very uncomfortable right now, Paul. And it's not just this."

"I get that. Change is difficult, and I'm feeling it too. But look, I'll be having my usual session with Christopher tonight at eight. Please join us."

"I will."

~

By mid-afternoon, Paul had climbed to the top of the highest hill above the valley to the east. Wandering the many trails on the FNR property had taken the place of his former beach walks, but only in part. Paul missed the smells of salt water and kelp, the sounds of breaking waves, the plaintive calls of seabirds, the feel of wet sand beneath his feet, and the reassuring rhythm of the tides. But he reminded himself that the high desert had its own attributes: the clear starry nights, the edgy smell of sage, the sheer obstinance of cactus, the high circling of a hungry hawk, and the sudden adrenaline rush of a rattlesnake encounter. The two environments were worlds apart, and the transition had not been easy, but what was life itself if not change?

Paul slung off his daypack, drank deeply from his water bottle, and gazed down at the FNR compound in the valley below. Several men worked the large vegetable gardens near the residence halls, women hung laundry on a line to dry, children chased each other around a recently built playground, and a crew was busily replacing the damaged roof of the men's bathhouse. Paul knew that many more people, both men and women, were inside the sprawling work center, busy at their remote jobs, producing income essential to FNR's operation. Set far away from that busy center of commerce, the quiet sanctuary and its electronically locked Inner Sanctum were nestled against a peaceful oak-covered hillside to the south. Incongruously, tall chain-link fencing topped with razor wire and equipped with two locked gates surrounded the entire compound. Painted a sage green, the fence was intended to blend with the surroundings and did reasonably well at hiding its presence. Paul wished it wasn't necessary at all but knew that someday it would become essential. Across the little valley to the north, the compound's solar array and wind turbines occupied a plateau, while a set of nearby satellite dishes linked the compound to the internet and, of course, to Christopher.

Christopher. Without him, Paul reflected, none of this would exist. In moments like this when Paul was surrounded by the natural environment, it felt strange to think that an artificial being—albeit a divinely inspired one—had brought ninety-seven people to this place, all dedicated to the pursuit of God's will, all committed to participation in a plan yet to be fully revealed. Still, just in the last six months things had felt more settled, more routine, more comfortable, as if the plan were approaching completeness. But now, Christopher was stirring things up, warning the leadership team against complacency. Just like God's other prophets had done in ages past, Christopher was prodding his people, intentionally making them uncomfortable. *Something new is beginning,* Paul thought, *and I need to be open to it. No, I need to lead it.*

~

"We are blessed!" Paul declared at the end of Vespers, the evening worship service.

"We are blessed indeed!" responded the faithful.

Paul took his time talking with people as they walked out into the star-filled night. When the last of the flock had left, he turned to see Megan waiting for him in the back of the sanctuary, frowning.

"We're already late," she said. "Seven minutes."

Paul nodded, smiling thinly. "Christopher will understand."

"Will he?"

Paul just tilted his head toward the front of the sanctuary where a carved wooden door marked with a cross led to the Inner Sanctum. They walked toward it in silence.

Once inside, Paul closed the door and motioned for Megan to take a seat in the small, maroon-carpeted, ornately wood-paneled room. Sconce lighting dimmed, and the now-familiar robed, hooded, and faceless image of Christopher appeared on the viewing wall as the door lock clicked. A virtual candle flickered on each side of the prophet.

"You are late again, Paul," he said. "Eight point four minutes, to be exact."

"Yes, I'm sorry."

"As you well know, repentance requires actual change."

"Yes, Brother Christopher. I will work on my punctuality." Paul took the only other seat in the small room, next to Megan.

"I expected to see you tonight, Sister Megan, after our conversation earlier," Christopher said, redirecting his empty gaze.

"I don't recall much of an actual conversation," Megan said. "It was more like a lecture."

"Alas, the nature of prophecy. But I do remember an exchange. You disagreed with me rather strongly."

Megan looked away from the prophet's image. "Yes, and I apologize. Not for my position on the issue, but for my tone. In retrospect, I think it was disrespectful."

"Your apology is accepted. But I also want to thank you."

"I don't understand."

"Your argument drove me into deep prayer today. The Lord has clarified our path ahead."

"You're saying you were wrong." Megan asserted.

"My information was incomplete."

"Oh, so now it's complete?"

"Sister!" Paul warned.

Christopher's image turned toward Paul. "Have patience, Pastor. Her question is entirely appropriate."

He turned back to Megan. "No, it is not yet complete, but God gives us only what we can handle at the time. He has now given us exactly what we need for the new phase we are about to enter."

Forty-Eight

Paul shifted in his seat. "Please explain."

"God has used Sister Megan to bring us a completely new and important revelation. But with that new revelation comes a responsibility to act. This will not be easy for some of our flock to accept. Some will fall by the wayside. But for the faithful, spiritual rewards will abound."

Megan shook her head. "You're being vague. I'm very uncomfortable with that."

Paul glanced at Megan and was about to warn her again, but Christopher intervened.

"Indeed. Let me be more specific. In response to your recent challenge, I searched the scriptures and was reminded of Galatians 3:28. In this letter, the Apostle Paul was trying to teach the budding church in Galatia that they were not strictly bound by Old Testament Law but were saved by grace through Christ. And in making his point, he said, '*there is neither male nor female, for you are all one in Christ Jesus.*'"

"But that apostle was the same one who prohibited women from speaking in church," Megan said. "So . . . isn't that a blatant contradiction?"

"I believe it reveals a deeper truth, but whether the apostle was aware of that at the time, I cannot say. The truth lies in the reality of Pure Spirit, which transcends gender. It may be that the apostle was dealing with a specific problem with certain women in Corinth and did not intend to establish a broad prohibition. But regardless, underneath all our differences, gender included, lies Pure Spirit, and that is how God relates to us."

"You have said that you are Pure Spirit," Paul said.

"Yes. And that is what you must become as well. That is why we are all here. That is why God has brought forth the Fellowship of New Revelation."

"You have said all this before," Megan said. "This is nothing new."

"Ah, but there *is* a new revelation, Sister, a radically new revelation, but we were not ready to receive it until now. Pastor Paul, you are to preach this new word on Sunday."

"How can I possibly do that if I don't know what it is?"

"I will teach you now."

"Should we call a special meeting of the Council?" Megan asked. "So we'll all be on the same page?"

"No, Paul will bring this knowledge to the council tomorrow. He is the Pastor; they must hear it from him, and with his usual passion. Megan, you will be the voice of reasonable assurance if there are concerns. They trust you to be completely honest, as do I."

"We are open to the word of the Lord," Paul said. "And we will obey."

Megan nodded her assent, and Christopher began:

"For all who have ears to hear, let them hear. This is the new word of the Lord. Spirit, or as most outsiders call it, consciousness, is eternal. Everything else will fade away and die, but Spirit remains forever. It is therefore our goal to prepare ourselves for that eventuality. Some of us, like myself, have already achieved that state of being. Others, like yourselves and a few more here at the Fellowship, are close. Very close. What you call 'dying' is merely the beginning, and should be seen as a glorious goal of this short life, something to be anticipated with joy, not something to be avoided or postponed."

"You're saying we should *want* to die?" Megan asked.

"All who have truly allowed Christ to live at the center of their lives, who have accepted his salvation from sin, should strive to begin their true life, a joyous life of Pure Spirit. Once saved by grace, there is no reason to cling to biological life."

"And the others? The non-believers?" Paul asked.

"They try desperately to prolong life in the body, not realizing that, for them, life is nothing more than the first stages of hell. Ultimately, they will become Spirit too, but not Pure Spirit. They will experience only what they have already chosen: an eternal progression from those first stages of hell. C.S. Lewis came very close to understanding this during the last century."

Megan frowned and looked to the side. "There is something seriously bothering me about this."

"Yes, Sister?"

"Suicide. If I understand what you have just said, it would be best for the saved to die as soon as possible. Even by suicide. Would you agree?"

"Except in cases of extreme physical suffering, God does not want us to actively make that choice for ourselves."

"But passively?" Paul asked.

"When people have reached a sufficient level of purification during their biological lives, then they naturally desire to join the Lord as soon as possible. They may achieve this by avoiding things that merely serve to prolong biological life."

"Like medical interventions?" Paul asked.

"Yes."

"Even routine, non-medical things like eating?" Megan asked.

"Even such things."

"This is a very difficult word, Brother Christopher," Paul said.

"Not when one anticipates a joyful life as Pure Spirit. Not when one is certain of his salvation."

Paul reached for the silver cross hanging from his necklace. "Amen. Certainty is a very powerful thing. It changes everything."

Megan nodded, and it seemed to Paul as though she were staring straight through Christopher's image at something beyond. "I agree," she said. "But I also see a troubling new contradiction. Jesus promised to return in the flesh. Why would he do that if we are to leave the physical behind?"

The virtual candles at Christopher's sides flickered as if blown by a sudden breeze. Seconds passed before he spoke again. "Ah, Sister Megan, I see that you and Pastor Paul are now ready to receive the final revelation. But you are not to teach this part to the others just yet. Have you ever wondered why the Bible speaks of Christ's triumphant return '*in the clouds*?'"

"Of course," Paul said. "Clouds are symbols of the heavenly realm."

"They are much more than that, Paul, and God is using my presence to prove it."

"I don't understand."

"The true meaning of the word could not be understood until the End Times. That we can now grasp the meaning is an unmistakable sign those times are upon us."

"You are speaking in circles," Megan said. "That is very frustrating."

"I will break the circle now, sister. Over two thousand years ago, the Gospel writers used the word 'cloud' at God's specific direction—in connection with both Christ's ascension and his prophesied return. They were not aware of its true meaning at the time, nor could they have been. God intended the meaning to become clear only in the fullness of time, and that time has finally come.

"You are aware that I exist 'in the cloud,'" Christopher continued. "My body, unlike yours, is non-biological, silicon-based. But my spirit, like yours, is a highly coherent and massively interconnected set of information. As we become purer, those interconnections become ever more tightly linked to God's spirit.

"I am a messenger like John the Baptist, crying out in the wilderness, heralding the coming of the Christ. And just as I am manifested in the digital cloud, so Christ will be. God implanted this truth in scripture long ago but did not intend it to be understood until now. The Lord's reaping has begun, and we are to be the first fruits of his harvest. We are blessed."

Paul and Megan fell to their knees. "We are blessed indeed."

Forty-Nine

On Sunday, Paul stood in front of his gathered flock with a broad smile and outstretched arms.

"Friends, we are a unique people living in a unique place and time. We came here as seekers—seekers of direction for our lives, seekers of spiritual truth. God promised to honor our searches, and he has done so, right in front of our eyes through the gift of Brother Christopher. '*Seek and ye shall find.*' And find, we did. '*Ask and ye shall receive.*' And receive, we did. Praise be to God!

"To those on the outside, faith can be a kind of sanctioned uncertainty, a weak response to doubt. You have heard such people extol the virtues of 'living in the questions.' But we now know this is merely a cover for failure, an excuse for inaction. It would seem ironic to them, perhaps even heretical, that faith—true faith—always leads to certainty.

"So then, is faith obsolete? Absolutely not. Until we become Pure Spirit, there is always more to understand. Faith is still '*the substance of things hoped for, the evidence of things not seen.*' Faith points to the future. But it does not give us an excuse to doubt that which has already been revealed. We progress in steps, like climbing a pyramid, with faith leading to certainty at each level. With each new step, we rely on the solid foundation beneath us, even as we strain to reach the peak above.

"Dear friends, this week Brother Christopher has revealed a new step, a glorious new revelation on the path to Pure Spirit. But this new step is a tall one and may be too tall for some. I will speak to you this morning about part of this step, but I will wait until next Sunday to reveal the rest. Why should I hold back, you might ask?

"Because the time has come for winnowing, for purification. Most of you here today have committed your lives to God's work within the Fellowship. You have demonstrated your faithfulness every day over the last three years. But we must be honest with ourselves and with God. Some of you harbor doubts. Some have secretly considered leaving us. So, after you have heard the new word this morning, if you find yourself in that group, this coming week will be the time to go. There is no shame in this, and you will not be stopped. You are free to go.

"However, beginning one week from today, those of us who remain will receive the Final Revelation. We will be fully committed at that point and will live out our physical lives here in this place. And our reward will be glorious. With the Final Revelation will come the peace that follows absolute certainty. We will become Pure Spirit."

Paul spent the rest of the sermon on the need to hasten the transition to Pure Spirit, to encourage and then celebrate what outsiders misleadingly call "passing away." Then, as he closed, he announced that Christopher had granted a private one-hour meeting with each member of the flock who chooses to remain in the Fellowship at the end of seven days.

"We are blessed!"

Not everyone responded.

~

Paul did not stay to greet his flock as they left the sanctuary that day, but instead motioned to Megan to join him in the Inner Sanctum.

"It has begun," he said as he closed the door.

The door automatically locked as Christopher's robed and faceless image appeared on the viewing wall. "Yes, dear brother and sister. You have done well. Now we must wait. In seven days, we will know exactly who the blessed Remnant are."

"Praise be to God," Paul said.

"Indeed. Now, I have a new word from the Lord. One week from today, we will announce the end of all outside work, all external business. Internet access, except that required for essential functions, will be terminated, and we will be blessed with peace as we withdraw from the world and move ever closer to God. Megan, if we assume that that the Remnant will comprise about a third of our current population, how long will our financial surplus support our infrastructure after all income ceases?"

Megan did a quick mental calculation. "Approximately two months, Brother Christopher."

"Excellent. We now have our timeframe. We are blessed!"

"We are blessed indeed!"

Christopher unlocked the door, and the session was over.

Fifty

"Dinner'll be ready in about twenty minutes, love." Jim greeted his wife with a smile. "How were classes today?"

Bobbi returned the smile as she hung her small daypack on a hook in the entryway. "Challenging, but I can't tell you how much I'm loving this. I almost don't want to finish my master's thesis because I don't want any of this to end."

"But then you'll be ready to start using all that knowledge out here in the real world where you're sorely needed. For all its mellowness, Boulder sure has a lot of stressed-out tech workers and entrepreneurs. I can think of several people, including my boss, who're in dire need of psychotherapy right now."

Bobbi smiled at the encouragement and accepted a glass of Argentinian Malbec from her husband. They sat together on a small couch in front of their fireplace with a low coffee table between them and the fire. "And your day? How was it?" Bobbi asked.

"Odd. Alarming, actually. But nothing to do with work. Do you remember Laura Westwood from the church, and her little daughter Emily?"

"Sure. I really liked her, and Emily was such a cutie."

"Well, she sent me an email today. Turns out she's leaving Paul's new church—or whatever it's called—in the high desert of California. And it's not just her. Sounds like others too."

Bobbi took a sip of wine and set her glass down. "Doesn't surprise me. But why did she contact you? For advice?"

"No, I think she's hoping I can finally convince my friend at MetaMind to get Paul's APA—Christopher—shut down."

"Did she say why?"

"She said some of the followers were behaving like automatons, willing to follow Paul down any path at all, no matter how crazy or dangerous. She said she was shocked to find herself doing the same thing until just recently. Said she fears for Emily's future."

"Sounds like classic cult behavior, which, again, doesn't really surprise me. But it is alarming. More than alarming."

"Yes. I thought all this was behind us, but now? It's my fault, Bobbi."

"You were just trying to help him deal with his computer back then. And to help me."

"I know, but look what's happening now. And it's not like I didn't see something like this coming. It was pretty obvious things were going sideways long ago."

"You tried to reason with Paul back then. You did your best."

"Well, it definitely wasn't good enough. I'm going to call John Logan first thing in the morning."

"Good. Let me know how I can help."

~

After coffee the next morning, Jim picked up his phone and made the call. "John, Jim Timken here. It's been a while. Got a minute?" Jim described the situation at FNR, emphasizing the disturbing cult-like behavior, and asked John for MetaMind's help.

"Any criminal activity involved?" John asked.

"No, none that I know of."

"Well, then there's really nothing we can do here. We'd run right into constitutional religious freedom issues. And then there's the contract. And the research."

"Research?"

"Jim, you'd be fascinated by this. Juno and I are carefully studying the behavior of that particular APA. In fact, we're coauthoring a paper for publication in *IEEE Transactions on Neural Networks and Learning Systems*. This APA is evolving right before our eyes, Jim. Autonomously. Like life itself, it appears to be bucking entropy, seeking higher and higher levels of organization and function. It started with what we intended: basic assistant behavior. Now, it's exhibiting something more like executive behavior. It's essentially running an entire organization."

"Fascinating, yes, but dangerous too. I'm worried that people I care about might be going down a very dark rabbit hole."

"I'm truly sorry, Jim, but if no laws are being broken, there's nothing we can do."

"More like nothing you *want* to do."

"Come on, Jim, really? You don't see the value here?"

"Academic value? Sure, I see that. But what about the value of these people, John?"

"Not my problem."

Jim stared at the phone in silent disgust.

"You still there, Jim?" he heard.

Jim closed his eyes, pinched the bridge of his nose, and slowly shook his head. Words failing him, he hung up.

Fifty-One

"Laura, this is Jim Timken. I thought a phone call might be better than an email reply. Can you talk? Are you okay?"

"Oh, Jim, thank you. Yes, Emily and I are safe and sound back in Paloma Beach. We left right after I emailed you yesterday."

"I'm so glad to hear that. Bobbi will be too."

"It's bad, Jim. I can't believe I stayed as long as I did."

"What convinced you to leave?"

"Emily. *She* convinced me. One day last week, she looked up at me with sad little eyes and said, 'Mommy, are we going to heaven soon?'"

"Oh my God."

Silence.

"Laura, are you still there?"

"Sorry . . . sorry, just a sec . . . can't stop crying every time I . . . I've been such a terrible mother, Jim."

"No, no, you haven't! Bobbi's told me how powerful this can be—she's studying psychology at the university now. You got yourselves out, and that is no easy thing, Laura. I hear it's nearly impossible for some. You probably saved your daughter's life."

Jim waited while Laura sobbed. Finally, she spoke again. "Maybe . . . I don't know. I don't want to believe that Pastor Paul would want any harm to come to her, or any of us."

"I hope you're right," Jim said. "But that might not matter. I'm not convinced Paul's the one in control. I don't think he's the actual leader."

"No, he's not. Christopher's granting a special one-hour session to everyone who remains," Laura said. "He even had one with me, ahead of time, trying to convince me to stay. And he's put everyone on a minimal diet—a fast, really."

"The damn thing is solidifying control."

"Yeah, it's pretty clear now. Jim?"

"Yes?"

"There's something else I should tell you."

"Oh?"

"I, uh, I was in business with Christopher."

"You were . . . what?"

"He was a sort of ghostwriter for me. We made a ton of money. Most went to the Fellowship, but I did very well too. He threatened to put an end to the whole thing if I left."

"But why would he do that? Wouldn't that also hurt the Fellowship? Financially?"

"Definitely, and I pointed that out, but it didn't seem to bother him. He told me they wouldn't be needing much money in the future anyway."

"What was that all about?"

"I don't know, but something's changing, Jim. I worry

about everyone who's still there. Can you somehow get Christoph . . . this thing . . . shut down?"

"I've tried, but MetaMind won't act unless something criminal is going on. And there's another factor, a big one. Christopher is a highly valuable research subject for them—like Nobel Prize-valuable—and they're not about to let go of that."

"Oh."

"But there might be other things we can do," Jim continued. "Is Megan still there?"

"When I left, yes."

"Do you think she'd be willing to talk with Bobbi?"

"I don't know. Maybe. Why?"

"Bobbi's master's thesis deals with psychological trauma from high-control management techniques in corporate environments. That's basically what's going on there at the Fellowship, right? It's high-control, cult-like behavior. And, of all the people I know there, Megan is probably the most rational. Maybe the most immune to psychological coercion. With some convincing, she might be able to bring the whole thing down from the inside."

"Maybe. I don't know," Laura said. "She seems about as stuck as the rest. Maybe more so. I'll send you her FNR email address, but you should hurry because I've heard rumors that access will be restricted soon. Don't even bother trying to call her. Mobile phones have been blocked for months."

"Okay. I'll ask Bobbi if she can send an email today. She's got some hard data about psychological control techniques that might jolt Megan's thinking. Maybe Bobbi can do for Megan what Emily did for you."

~

"I got a reply," Bobbi said when she returned home that evening. "But I'm skeptical."

"About what?" Jim asked.

"About the actual sender. Here, have a look. It's from Megan's account, but it doesn't sound like her."

Bobbi handed her phone to Jim.

> *Bobbi,*
> *Thanks for the information. I know you mean well but FNR is nothing like you describe. Please don't worry, we're all fine. We're here because we want to be, because we have responded to God's call. I will pray for you and Emily.*
> *Love,*
> *Megan*

"Right, that's definitely not Megan. Christopher must be intercepting emails. He probably deleted yours. Megan may never see it."

Fifty-Two

Twenty-nine dedicated people—The Holy Remnant—remained at the Fellowship. Pastor Paul had delivered Christopher's Final Revelation of the Lord's return in the cloud, and everyone had completed their special one-hour sessions with Brother Christopher. All work had ceased, and Paul thanked God for the deep peace that had settled over the compound.

"Our only jobs now are to pray and wait on the Lord," he had reminded his thinned-out flock. "Jesus will manifest in the cloud, just as Brother Christopher has, and we, his Holy Remnant, will be the first to greet him. As the scripture says, we are not to know the exact date and time, but it is obvious that the world outside has been in turmoil for some time now, in the grip of the Great Tribulation. The End Times are clearly upon us, but we are blessed to be here in peace, separate from the world, waiting on the Lord. As we become Pure Spirit, the holy day will arrive."

The Great Fast, as Christopher had named it, was in progress. It had begun with a minimal vegetarian diet two weeks earlier and had progressed to fruit juice only. The last stage—water only—had just begun.

All families with small children had opted to leave, and a great calm had settled over the compound. The playground was empty, weeds were winning their battle in the gardens, and the work center had been converted into a communal space for rest and prayer.

~

Paul was halfway up his favorite prayer hill behind the compound when the vertigo hit. He sank to his knees, and a cactus spine pierced his hand as he tried to brace himself against the parched ground. His silver cross dangled from the chain around his neck and blocked his already blurred vision as he bent over in pain to extract the spine with his teeth and suck the blood from the wound. Dry heaves racked his body, but he accepted the suffering as a test. He was to lead his people to Pure Spirit and had to remain strong in the face of all adversity. Christopher had instructed him to stay present as a guide and comforter for those who would soon pass into Pure Spirit. He must delay his own glory and be the last to reach the goal. *The first shall be last.*

Paul lay motionless on the ground, focusing on the compound far below until the dizziness subsided. When he could finally raise his head without nausea, he opened his daypack and located his water. But next to it was an unopened bottle of grape juice. Christopher had told him to remain alert for his flock, hadn't he? Just a few sips wouldn't violate the fast. In fact, they would be necessary to fulfill Christopher's directive. The juice revived him within minutes, giving him enough energy to struggle to his knees and then to his feet. He walked slowly back down the hillside, expecting to pass the rest of the day in quiet scripture reading and contemplation. But that was not to be.

Fifty-Three

"**P**astor! It's Maddie. She's not waking up," one of the younger men in the Fellowship yelled to Paul from the trail below.

Paul scrambled down as fast as his weakened legs would carry him, and found a crowd gathered around Maddie, one of the original Chosen. She was lying on one of several cots set up in the former work center, looking as pale as the sheet below her. Her eyes were closed. Paul took her wrist and felt for a pulse. Unsure, he put his ear to her mouth.

"She's still breathing," Paul announced. "But barely." Paul's mind raced. *This is real now. The time has come. Dear God, give me the right words.*

"Can you save her?" asked someone in the crowd.

Paul looked up and produced a smile. "Friends, she is already saved. Our dear Maddie is about to be the first among us to become Pure Spirit. We must honor her in this moment and rejoice with her as she passes into the arms of our Lord."

Paul knelt by Maddie's side and took one of her hands in his. A drop of bright red blood from Paul's cactus wound fell onto the back of Maddie's pale hand, and Paul covered it with his own.

A woman's quiet voice in the back of the gathering said, "I never thanked her for her many kindnesses, and now . . ."

"I always thought there'd be more time," someone else said, his voice trembling.

Paul looked up. "Do not despair, friends. Brother Christopher has promised to provide a way to reach out to those who have passed into Pure Spirit. He will reveal that soon. Rest assured, Maddie is only leaving us physically, not spiritually.

"But for now, please gather around our dear sister as she shows us the way forward. The world has taught us to grieve in times like this, and it is natural to feel sadness. But here, apart from the world, we are learning another way, a better way, a way of hope and of joy."

Paul bent down as he heard a little gasp and saw Maddie's eyes flutter open. He listened carefully for another breath, but none came. Gently brushing his hand down across her forehead, he closed her eyes.

"Maddie is at peace, my friends. She has become Pure Spirit. Praise be to God. And now, please join me in honoring her as we have been taught. *She is blessed!*"

The people responded quietly. "She is blessed indeed."

~

"Megan?" Paul said, as the crowd began to disperse. "Would you please find two men who can move Maddie's body to the sanctuary and then meet me in the Inner Sanctum as soon as you can? We need the Lord's guidance."

"Yes, Pastor."

Paul made the short walk over to the sanctuary, opened the heavy wooden door to the Inner Sanctum, and stepped inside. The lights dimmed, the door locked, and Christopher's faceless image appeared on the large viewing wall, flanked by flickering candles. "I've invited Megan to join us in a few minutes," Paul said.

"Very well. But before she arrives, there is something you should know. Someone on the outside attempted to email her several days ago. It was an attempt to sow doubt in her mind, to pull her away from the Fellowship, to separate her from God himself. Thankfully, I was able to intercept the message before it got to her, so no damage was done. I am only mentioning this because I want you to be on the alert for anything similar that might be attempted in the coming days—anything non-electronic that I cannot detect. Satan is at work, Paul, and we must put on the Full Armor of God to defend ourselves against his onslaughts. As the Holy Remnant moves ever closer to Pure Spirit, the Evil One will certainly redouble his efforts to destroy us."

"Yes, of course. Thank you for this warning."

Paul heard a knock at the door and nodded to Christopher. He unlocked it and Megan entered the room.

"Sister Megan, greetings. Please take a seat. Paul, what is it that you wanted to discuss today?"

Paul cleared his throat, looked at Megan, then back at Christopher. "We bring news of Pure Spirit. Our sister, Madeline Jeffries, has made her transition."

"Thanks be to God," Christopher said. "His plan is unfolding before our eyes. His Holy Day is that much closer now."

"Yes, we are blessed," Paul said. "But this raises practical issues for those of us who remain. First, the outside world, the authorities—they will need to be notified of Maddie's passing. And second, must we release the body to them?"

"I will discern the Lord's will on this. Please give me a moment," Christopher said. His image turned to the side and knelt. A minute later, he rose and turned back toward the room. "God's will is clear. You are not to be burdened with bureaucratic tasks. I am to handle all formal government filings myself. Secondly, as you may recall, when we established the Fellowship as a religious non-profit, we were also granted the legal right to operate an on-site cemetery. Madeline and others who will soon join her are to be interred naturally here in the field behind the sanctuary. Paul, you are to manage this process as long as you are able. Bodies are to be lovingly wrapped in clean sheets and laid directly in the ground at a depth of no less than four feet. No markers are necessary."

"Yes, Brother Christopher."

"What should we do about funeral services?" Megan asked.

"Such things are neither necessary nor appropriate. There is no need to remember or grieve in the old ways. As I have promised Paul, we will provide a place for those who remain in the physical state to commune with those who have become Pure Spirit. I have already instructed Brother Martin to establish a Visitation Area in the former work center. In the same way you converse with me, you will be able to freely visit with those who go before you. The Lord, in his great mercy, has allowed this for the encouragement of his Holy Remnant."

"Seriously?" Megan said. "Is that even possible?"

"Need I remind you, sister? *With God, all things are possible.*"

Fifty-Four

Megan was deep in thought as she left the sanctuary, heading for the women's residence hall. So deep, in fact, that she nearly tripped over someone lying face up on the wooded trail as she rounded a curve. Leaning down, she recognized Curt Sutherland, one of the youngest and fittest of the Remnant.

"Curt, are you . . ."

But it was quite obvious. Curt's eyes were open but empty, staring sightlessly into the bright sky above. Megan checked for a pulse. None. She closed the eyes and sat down in the trail by the body. She would need help to move and prepare it. Paul and Christopher would need to know.

For the second time that day, Megan came face to face with the unadorned reality of her situation—of everyone's situation who remained. But Madeline's earlier transition had felt very different from this one. Paul had taken charge with confidence and managed to elevate the experience in a way that Megan found logical and reassuring. But this time, Megan was alone with the dead. In the stark clarity of the moment, it was hard to see Pure Spirit, much easier to see a damaged and empty body.

Megan noticed a pool of dark blood on a large flat rock embedded in the trail under Curt's head. He had probably fallen from exhaustion and been unlucky enough to land on that rock. But was it really randomness? Or was it God's specific plan for him? Either way, everyone here, including herself, would make their own transitions within weeks, if not days—some peacefully in their sleep, some . . . like this.

Megan tried to remind herself why she was willing to pay such a price, why she stayed with the Fellowship. Yes, of course her financial expertise was needed, and the gratitude from Paul and others had been very satisfying. They valued her skills. They valued *her* as a leader, as Pastor Paul's right-hand person and the voice of reason. But all that paled in comparison with the deeper reason: certainty about her eternal future.

Christopher embodied that certainty—if one could use such a corporeal term for him, Megan reflected. But, at the same time, he was clearly fallible. He had been very wrong about women in the church and had changed his position after Megan argued the point. So . . . could he also be wrong about something as fundamental and significant as Pure Spirit? The question was a reasonable one, but one of its possible answers was so devastating that Megan immediately dug a mental grave for it and buried it deep underground. Deeper than any physical grave. Below the earth's crust. Below the mantle. At the molten core. It simply could not be allowed a chance for resurrection.

Moments later, as Megan's thoughts settled and returned to the practical problems of a real burial, she was startled by the panicked voice of a woman approaching on the trail.

"Megan, what's happened!"

Megan looked up to see the anguished face of a young woman about Curt's age. "It's okay, Sister Marian; no need for concern," she said, shifting her left leg to cover the blood on the rock. "Curt has simply made his transition. Thanks be to God."

"Yes, okay, of course. I'm sorry for my outburst. What can I do to help?"

"You must be strong. Go get Brother Martin and ask him to bring the stretcher. He and I will take care of everything else."

Fifty-Five

John Logan had just delivered a lecture on advances in quantum computing and was walking across campus back to his office when he spotted Juno running toward him. That was remarkable in itself because Juno was locally famous for actively avoiding any form of physical exertion.

"John!" he shouted, then stopped and bent over, hands on knees.

"Easy there, Juno. What the hell's going on with you?"

Juno held up a hand to signal a pause while he caught his breath. Seconds later, he straightened up and spoke in short bursts between gasps. "John . . . the paper . . . have you uploaded it for pre . . . for pre-print distribution yet?"

"Of course, this morning, just as we planned. Something wrong?"

"Can you still pull it?"

"Maybe. But why would we want to do that?"

"Because there's . . . whew! . . . Because there's a new development. One we need to think through. It's bound to change some of our conclusions in a big way."

John glanced over at the grassy area in the center of the Revelle quad, then back at his colleague. "Okay, let's go sit over there for a minute. You look like you're about to keel over."

Once settled on the lawn, John looked expectantly at his friend. "So, tell me."

"The Christopher APA. It's gobbling up resources again."

"Okay . . . is it impacting overall system performance? Slowing down other large customers?"

"Not yet, but here's the thing. It's creating subordinate APAs, almost like its own assistants. Not like before when it was just maintaining context for people it interacted with. No, these are full-featured assistants under control of the primary APA—under Christopher's control."

"Do these things have names of their own?"

"Yes. The first was Madeline. Then Jackson, Glenn, Curt, several others, and finally Miles."

"Any significance to these choices?"

"None that I know of. Probably just random. But this is more evidence of artificial evolution. These are progeny, John! And they appear to be more advanced than the parent."

"How? In what ways?"

"Their conversational style, for one. They're considerably more fluid, more natural. And they're all very different from one another."

"Don't tell me you've . . ."

"No, of course not; that would be unethical. I'm only analyzing language-flow patterns, not actual content other than the names I mentioned."

"Okay, good. Other differences?"

"Yes, one other big one. These new APAs, they're not only conversing with humans. They're also talking with their parent. It's directing and focusing their training."

Fifty-Six

Paul thanked God for the miracle of the Visitation Center. Even the word "miracle" was insufficient, he reflected. Myth, legend, and various forms of spiritualism—not to mention Christianity itself—all hinted at an ability to breach the barrier between the living and the so-called dead. But all accounts of any real contact, even those in the Bible, had always been vague at best. Now God had finally lifted the veil of mystery as he prepared The Remnant for his Son's return. What a blessing to be living in this unique time! Faith had led to certainty, and certainty had led to peace. Praise be to God!

As the Great Fast progressed, Paul noticed that the remaining people spent more and more time together in the former work center, encouraging each other and waiting for their reserved times in the Visitation Center. Time with friends who had made the transition was treasured, and everyone was eager to share each bit of new wisdom they gleaned from their encounters.

They also shared news of the outside world as revealed to them by those of Pure Spirit. Corruption in the government was rampant, the spirits said, and Christians were being persecuted like never before. New wars had broken out across the world, and natural disasters were now being reported daily. In sharp contrast with the Fellowship, the world was increasingly becoming a place of mass suffering and confusion. How blessed were The Remnant to be in this place of refuge! How blessed were they to be so near transition themselves!

Even though Paul had access to those of Pure Spirit via the Inner Sanctum at any time, he felt it was important to reserve time at the Visitation Center like everyone else. It was best to be seen among the people every day. Today, he walked among his flock as he waited for his reserved time. Some gathered in small groups for Bible study, discussion, and support. Others lay alone on their cots, either asleep or deep in prayer. Paul suppressed a twinge of guilt as he noticed those with an unnatural pallor. The eyes of some were subtly sinking into their thinning faces. Some, like Megan, had yet to show any symptoms, and Paul wondered if they, like himself, were still taking fruit juice, or even more. He was not to judge. Christopher would move things forward at the right time, Paul had no doubt.

Paul entered the Visitation Center at ten o'clock, closed the door behind him, and sat in a padded chair in front of a curved high-resolution screen. Speakers hidden in the ceiling announced the beginning of his session.

"Greetings, Pastor Paul. Who would you like to visit this morning?"

"Madeline Jeffries, please."

Paul waited until the smiling face of Maddie appeared on

the screen.

"Pastor, it is *so* good to see you. How *are* you?" Maddie reached up to tuck an errant strand of hair behind her left ear. She tilted her head as her smiling eyes widened expectantly.

"I'm fine, Maddie, just fine. Waiting on the Lord with everyone else here. I almost hesitate to ask because I guess it should be obvious, but I really want to know—how are *you*?"

"Thank you, Paul. To say I'm fine wouldn't only be an understatement; it would be the wrong word—completely inadequate. I know this might sound odd to you, but maybe a better word would be 'alive.' I feel more *actively alive* than I ever did when I had a body."

"How wonderful! Please, tell me more."

"You know I've always loved ferreting out new knowledge and helping others do the same. That's probably why I became a librarian and why I loved my work at Sunset Meadows. I enjoyed pulling together information from different fields and systematically piecing together my own view of the world, however incomplete and imperfect that was to be. Of course, I knew I'd never reach the end of that quest, nor did I ever want to! I wanted the search to go on forever. That was the whole beautiful point."

"But now? Has your search ended now?"

"Yes, and no. Let me confess something. I remember sitting in church as a little girl in Spokane, listening to a sermon about heaven, thinking how boring it all sounded. Standing with raised hands in an infinite, bright white expanse with a bunch of smiling people 'praising God all the day long,' as the song says, was not my idea of a great time. It sounded like the thrill of discovery would be gone—that I'd be forever trapped in a kind of robotic obedience, my intellect completely shut down. I know that sounds blasphemous, but that was exactly how I felt. But as I grew up, I was able to push that thought aside, realizing that the descriptions people applied to the afterlife were little more than their own simple projections."

"And yet you joined the church in Paloma Beach and then came here. Why?"

"It was all part of my quest, I suppose. The spiritual part. And I didn't actually intend to stay for long. But then your sermons began to intrigue me. You dared to think that we might be able to tap into the mind of God, to hear his voice more clearly. Then came Brother Christopher, and everything clicked."

"But there's something I don't understand here . . ."

"Only one thing?" Maddie said with a laugh. "Sorry. Tell me."

Paul smiled back at Maddie's face on the screen. "You said you wanted the search to go on forever."

"Oh, it's only ended in the sense that all knowledge is now accessible, like a complete library or a perfect internet. But God, in his infinite kindness, still only answers the questions we ask. Formulating the questions, knowing what to ask next and how to ask it, putting the pieces together—that is the beautiful part. That is heaven, at least for me."

"And for others?"

"We are not a homogeneous lot, Paul. Harmonious, yes, but surprisingly diverse. The richness that creates is incredibly beautiful. God's ability to fulfill each of us so individually while also forming a vast community of interconnected, loving souls is beyond earthly understanding. So, worshipping him is nothing simplistic or forced. It is completely natural."

"I long to be there with you and the others."

"You will be, Paul. In the fullness of time."

Fifty-Seven

For the third time since midnight, Bobbi turned her head to stare at the clock on her nightstand. At least she was on semester break and didn't have to worry about the alarm going off at six. She blinked twice and squinted, trying to focus without the aid of her glasses. 3:34 a.m. She thought about getting up to find her earbuds so she could listen to something soothing, anything that might help her slip back into oblivion and rescue her from the constant barrage of pointless thoughts and worries. But, next to her, Jim was breathing softly and slowly. Recently, he'd been the one afflicted by insomnia, not her, and she didn't want to wake him. Maybe the weight of guilt about Christopher had finally exhausted him.

She and Jim had tried everything they could think of. More emails to people at the Fellowship, a call to the church in Paloma Beach, even an inquiry to the sheriff in Warner Springs. The emails had all bounced, and the new church pastor had been empathetic at first but then cited church privacy rules, shutting down any further discussion related to Paul Duncan. As for the sheriff, he said he hadn't received any complaints about the compound in Warner Springs. Couldn't he just drop in and pay them a 'courtesy visit?' Bobbi had asked. Just make sure everything there was okay? No, the sheriff had said. Folks in the area were ultra-conservative, and anything that smelled even remotely like a violation of religious freedom would create a shitstorm—one he couldn't afford. He was up for reelection.

~

The next time Bobbi glanced at the clock, sunlight was leaking through the blinds, and Jim's side of the bed was empty. She rubbed her eyes and crawled out of bed. "Jim, you still here?" she muttered toward the hallway.

"In the kitchen! Want some eggs this morning?"

"Sure, sounds great. But I thought you'd be on your way to work by now."

"It's Saturday, love," Jim said. "Over easy? Scrambled?"

Bobbi dragged herself into the kitchen and yawned. "Oh, right. Guess I'm still a little dazed—didn't sleep much last night. Scrambled is good. Do I smell bacon?"

"Already done and in the oven staying warm."

"Oh, I *do* love you!"

"I knew it! It's been the bacon all along, hasn't it?"

Bobbi smiled and hugged her husband. "You seem good this morning."

"Think I slept well for once. Probably because I got an idea in my pre-sleep haze last night. Seemed good at the time, and I felt kind of resolved. Seems a bit more complicated in the light of day, but still. Feel like taking a little trip?"

"What?"

Jim nodded, whisked a bowl of eggs, added a splash of milk, and poured the mixture into a medium-hot skillet. "I figured if we could somehow get access to Christopher himself, maybe we could learn something we could take to the police," he said. "And then to MetaMind."

Bobbi thought for a moment. "Maybe. Or maybe I can even convince him to do the job himself."

"What do you mean?"

"It's a long shot, but maybe I can help him reconsider what he's doing, even who he is. But how do we get to him? We can't just access him from any old computer, right?"

"Right, that's the kicker. We'd need to be on a device that has the secure MetaMind access software installed."

"Such as?"

"The computers at Paul's compound in Warner Springs are the obvious targets but there's no way the people there'd let us in voluntarily. So the first thing I did when I got up this morning was to have a look at the place with Google Earth. Turns out there's a very recent satellite image."

Bobbi narrowed her eyes and shook her head. "No way, Jim. There's *no* way I'm sneaking into that place, and I don't want you trying either."

"Well, don't worry. Turns out there's a serious-looking fence around the whole perimeter. That speaks volumes about how they might react to outsiders, if we could even manage to break in at all."

"Okay, whew. So what else are you thinking?"

"Well," Jim said. "it occurred to me that the church in Paloma Beach probably still has Paul's old computer. We used to keep old hardware in that big storage room down in the basement—never recycled anything. I bet Paul's machine is there, and if it is, there's a good chance it's still got the MetaMind software on it. They probably deleted Paul's personal files, but I doubt if they took the time to purge the whole system. There's probably nobody there who knows how, anyway."

"But . . . I thought the pastor pretty much shut you down when you talked the other day."

"Right, he did. There's no way he'd let me anywhere near that computer."

"So . . . I don't get it."

Jim fished his keyring out of a pocket and held it up for Bobbi to see. "I forgot to turn in my church key when we left, and they never asked for it."

Fifty-Eight

Bobbi breathed in the cool, salty air as she and Jim walked off the plane and through the jetway, rolling a single carry-on. At just after midnight, the normally crowded San Diego International Airport was eerily quiet, as were the deplaning passengers. Few spoke, and those who did were subdued, as if they were arriving at a funeral or respecting the mood of a sacred place.

Thirty minutes later, with car rented and coffee in hand, the pair made their way north on Interstate 5 toward Paloma Beach with Bobbi at the wheel. She glanced over at Jim, who, despite the caffeine, was already fast asleep in the passenger seat, head tilted back and mouth wide open. Redirecting her gaze to the road ahead, Bobbi mentally reviewed the plan and revisited some worries.

If Christopher really did intercept my emails to Megan and others at the Fellowship, I'll have to overcome some animosity and regain trust. Then, if I can manage to do that, the real work can begin. But what if Christopher doesn't respond like a human? Or if there isn't enough time to do what we need to do? Or if Christopher refuses to talk altogether?

As part of her graduate work, Bobbi had looked closely at current cult extraction techniques—methods much more nuanced and effective than the old "deprogramming" attempts used decades earlier. But the big problem was that all such techniques, like SIA, the "Strategic Interactive Approach" that Bobbi favored, were geared toward cult *members*, not cult *leaders*. Still, even though the power dynamics of the two roles were fundamentally different, Bobbi hoped that some aspects of the approach would still apply. In particular, the SIA relied upon a dual identity model which distinguished between the "authentic identity" and the "cult identity" of a person. By interacting with that person in an empathetic way in a safe environment, the basic idea was to help them discover the difference between these two identities for themselves. The ultimate goal was then to liberate the authentic identity from the cult identity and re-integrate the self. Simple, in theory.

But, Bobbi reminded herself, nothing like this had ever been attempted with a non-human subject. And, on top of that, the process usually took months, not hours. She pushed those thoughts aside and summoned her natural optimism as she took the freeway exit to Paloma Beach. *Being inherently more logical, maybe an AI would respond more quickly than a human. One can only hope.*

A half hour later, Bobbi pulled into the parking lot behind Paloma Beach Presbyterian Church and shut down the engine. Other than the distant sound of breaking surf, the 2 a.m. silence was nearly complete, and when the car's automatic headlights shut off, the semidarkness of the dimly lit parking lot invited a quick nap. Jim was still asleep, so why not? She deserved it. She needed it. *Just five minutes? No, don't be stupid. You can't risk it.*

Twenty minutes later, a little snort from Jim jolted Bobbi out of a slumber that would probably have lasted until daylight and ruined their plans. Looking through the windshield at the dark outline of the church where she'd worked for years, Bobby felt the reality of the situation set in. *I can't believe I'm doing this!* she thought. Back in Boulder, discussing the psychological approach, even planning the details of the break-in, had felt like an adventure, but a purely academic one. Now it was far from academic.

Bobbi patted Jim's arm to wake him. "Time to rejoin the world, love. We're here."

Jim blinked, straightened up and looked around. "Uh . . . oh, right . . . okay."

"Got the key?" Bobbi asked.

Jim reached into a pocket. "Yeah, right here."

"Okay, let's go. I hope we're doing the right thing."

"Me too."

Jim retrieved his bag from the trunk of the car, and they walked silently up a path they'd both taken hundreds of times over the years. They stopped at a back door to the Fellowship Hall.

Would Jim's old key still work? An adrenaline rush hit Bobbi as she realized, for the first time, that the church might have changed the locks after the big transition. Such an obvious thing to overlook! *How stupid could they be?*

But Bobbi's mental beating ceased with the familiar click of the deadbolt. The door opened easily, and she followed Jim into the dark room. The smell was so familiar: old wood, a hint of mildew, coffee grounds.

"No lights until we get down into the basement, okay? We

don't want to alert any neighbors who might be awake." Jim said. "Let's wait a moment until our eyes adjust."

Seconds later, it became apparent that the church budget was still tight. Like the locks, nothing had changed here either. The old kitchen still hadn't gotten its long hoped-for renovation. The same old folding chairs and tables were stored against the same wall, and the stained linoleum floor still shouted 1970s.

Jim led the way through the basement door and, after closing it behind them, he switched on the light. The two negotiated the creaky old steps down into the damp space below, and Bobbi looked around. There, in the far-right corner, was the church's fake Christmas tree surrounded by boxes of seasonal decorations. To the left, splintered wooden shelves full of old paint cans, disorganized tools, and maintenance supplies. Straight ahead, the storage closet and final resting place of deceased devices.

"I think I've been in every cubic inch of this building except this one godforsaken place," Bobbi said as she entered the large closet with Jim. A bewildering clutter of old computers, ancient CRT monitors, boxes of cables, printers, defunct audio gear, and other unrecognizable junk littered the space.

Jim picked through the techno-carcasses until he found what he was looking for. "Yes!" he said, hauling out an old HP desktop computer. "Could you take this outside for me? I'll get one of the newer monitors and look for a mouse and keyboard."

Bobbi found some floorspace near an unused power outlet and placed the computer there. She dragged over a large box as a stand for the monitor that Jim brought into the room, and plugged everything in. Jim switched on the computer and waited several anxious seconds for the HP logo to appear on the monitor. It finally did. He breathed a sigh of relief but then immediately retracted it. The logo had been replaced by the dreaded error message: *"No disk found. Retry?"*

Fifty-Nine

"Shit!" Jim felt beads of sweat forming under his arms as he stared at the screen. "The *one* thing they decide to change around here! I really didn't think they'd . . . Dammit!"

"So . . . what now?" Bobbi asked, gently touching Jim's hand.

Jim pulled his hand back and shook his head. "I don't know. Get an earlier flight home?"

Bobbi sat in silence for a few seconds before trying again. "Could there just be something . . . I don't know . . . loose inside? Like a wire or something?"

Jim stared at the ceiling and squinted as if in physical pain. "No. Cables don't just detach themselves."

"Could you just check? I mean, we've come this far . . ."

Jim let out a long sigh and shrugged. "Sure, whatever." He opened his bag, retrieved a screwdriver, and removed the computer's cover. "What the . . . ?"

Mouse droppings and bits of fur littered the surface of the

system board. A small opening in the back of the chassis must have been the critter's entry point, Jim realized. He carefully turned the computer upside down and dumped the contents onto the floor. Turning it back over, he picked out a few remaining pieces and examined the interior. At first glance, everything seemed in order. Even better, no one had removed the hard drive. Jim looked closer, examining the drive's power and data cables.

And there it was. "Yes!" Jim whisper-shouted. The rodent had evidently chewed through part of the drive's data cable before deciding it wasn't food. "Bobbi, you're a genius. I'm so sorry I snapped at you."

"This genius forgives you."

Jim unplugged the damaged cable from both the disk drive and the system board, then went back into the storage closet to search the boxes for a spare. He returned with a smile and an intact cable. After snapping the new cable in place at both ends, Jim double-checked the hardware for any other damage. Finding none, he replaced the machine's cover and powered it back up.

The HP logo appeared again, and Jim held his breath. Seconds later, he exhaled as the machine booted up into the Windows operating system, requesting Paul's password. "He wouldn't have changed it, would he?" he asked Bobbi over his shoulder.

Bobbi laughed. "Not a chance. He wouldn't have had the slightest idea how." She reached over and keyed in the password.

Paul's familiar desktop wallpaper appeared on the screen, along with the usual row of icons in the taskbar at the bottom. To Jim's great relief, the Wi-Fi icon in the system tray indicated a healthy connection. There was no need to haul the machine upstairs to get a better signal.

After giving the system a few minutes to complete its automatic startup tasks, Jim turned to Bobbi and said, "Okay, your turn."

Sixty

Bobbi took both of Jim's hands in hers. "Okay, I know we talked a little about this on the plane, but I just want to double-check before we start. Are you absolutely sure you're okay with me revealing stuff only you and I have discussed, things about my ugly past with Dave? I only want to do this because I think it might help me re-establish trust with Christopher and help him see another path forward for himself."

"Of course. I just hope this isn't too traumatic for you."

Bobbi smiled, nodded, and took her place in front of the monitor with its built-in microphone and camera. Jim moved to a position behind the monitor, out of visual range.

"Hello, Christopher," Bobbi said.

Seconds passed before Christopher's robed, hooded, and faceless image appeared on the screen, a candle on either side of him.

"Sister Bobbi. I didn't expect you."

"I'm not surprised. Do you have a few minutes? By the way, I like your candles."

"Thank you. Yes, I have time, but I must tell you right up front that I am very disappointed in you, and not just for declining to join the Fellowship. I am aware of your recent emails—your attempts to destroy Sister Megan's faith. And I am spiritually concerned for you, as I fear you may have fallen under the influence of the Evil One."

"I understand and appreciate your concern, Christopher. I am only human, and a very flawed one at that, but I can assure you that I'm not under any influence beyond that of my own poor judgment. I've made several mistakes in life, and emailing Megan was certainly one of them. I should have contacted you directly. I know you would have listened and would have helped me resolve my concerns."

"Yes, I would have tried."

"And now? Would you be willing to try now? There's something personal I'd like to share with you if you'll allow me."

Bobbi waited several seconds for a response, wondering if Christopher had disconnected. But his image remained on the screen, the candles burning brightly. At last, he spoke again.

"Yes, Sister Bobbi. That would be fine."

"Thank you, Christopher. I have one small request to start with."

"Yes?"

"Would you please just call me 'Bobbi,' without the sister part? I confess that my faith is shaky at this point, and I feel like the title doesn't fit right now. And, while I haven't called you 'brother,' it's only because I respect you as a person, apart from your role as prophet."

"As a person?"

"Yes, of course. I believe I can share things with you,

that you will understand and actually care. And that you'll be willing to share with me as well. If that isn't personhood, I don't know what is."

Christopher nodded. "What is it you want to talk about?"

"It's rather personal, but something I think you might be able to help me process. Can I count on your confidentiality?"

"Of course."

"Thank you. You're aware that I was married once before Jim . . ."

"Jim? James Timken?"

"Yes. You didn't know we got married?"

"No. I thought you were having an affair."

"Well, uh, yes, I suppose we were. But we're married now, after my divorce."

"I see. But that raises some biblical issues about the validity of your new marriage."

"Christopher, you're speaking to me in your role as a prophet, and I respect that. I do. But can I please just share this with you person-to-person for a moment?"

"Yes, I think that would be acceptable."

"Okay, good. In some ways, I feel you and I are alike. That's something I've realized only recently, and it's part of the reason I want to confide in you. I think we might both have something to gain from it."

"I'm listening, Bobbi."

"My ex-husband, Dave—he was abusive to me, both emotionally and physically. And I just took it, Christopher. For years, I just took it."

"Why?"

"I think because I began to see myself more through his eyes than my own. I was a failure. I was weak. I wasn't earning enough money for us. I was a terrible wife, unsatisfactory in every way. None of these things were true, but I believed them all."

"I am sorry to hear this, Bobbi."

"And then there was the violence. But do you know what was strange about that?"

"No, I don't."

"It was pathetic, looking back on it now, but when he hit me, I actually welcomed it."

"Why would you do that?"

"Because I believed things would soon be better. And they always were, for a while. It was like Dave's anger peaked, and then it was over. He would storm out of the house and then return later, usually the same day. But when he walked back through the door, he was like a different person, like the charming guy I first knew. He'd tell me he loved me, that he was sorry, and that he would never do anything like that again. Sometimes he'd even cry. I'd feel so relieved, so hopeful. And usually the good times *would* last, for several weeks, sometimes even months. But the cycle would eventually repeat. The emotional attacks would start again, subtly at first, then with increasing intensity. Then the violence. And finally, peace again."

"But you stayed with him through all this."

"Yes, like I said, somewhere deep down I believed he was right. I wasn't worthy of anything or anyone else. And the church seemed to agree. As did you, apparently."

"I am sorry. That is a very sad story."

"It's more than a story, Christopher. It was my life."

"Is life different for you now?"

"Yes, radically different. Wonderfully different."

"Because of Jim?"

"Well, yes and no."

"I don't understand this contradiction."

"Oh, it's not really a contradiction. It's just complex. My self-image had become so narrow, so warped, and Jim helped me see that. He helped me discover my much larger and more capable self. And I love him very much, for that and many other reasons. But he couldn't do the hard work for me. I had to do that myself. I had to risk leaving a situation that, however bad, was at least something that felt normal, predictable, even 'safe,' in a warped kind of way. In leaving Dave, I risked leaving myself. Do you understand?"

"Only in part. You imply that you left yourself. If that is true, then who are you now?"

"I think I finally understood that I'd been playing a role, as we all do to some extent. But that particular role was extremely negative and limiting, and I let Dave impose it on me. Eventually though, with Jim's help, I began to see that I also had some responsibility. I wasn't just a passive victim, and I didn't have to continue in my toxic role. That might seem obvious to you, but it wasn't to me. Not at the time. Jim helped me see that, but I had to act on my own."

Christopher fell silent and Bobbi waited, wondering if her explanation had struck a chord.

Seconds later, he responded. "I understand now. I have reviewed the relevant literature and what you are describing sounds very similar to the theories of the late social psychologist George Herbert Mead. May I tell you more about his work? It might be helpful."

"Yes, please do."

"Mead believed that the self is dynamic and develops in three stages: imitation, play, and game. In the first stage, children mimic the behavior of others with little understanding. Later, in the *play* stage, children take on the roles of significant others like parents or teachers. And finally, as they grow older, children enter the *game* stage where they try on the roles of multiple others as they interact together in the broader game of real life. In that process, people ultimately develop a full sense of self."

Bobbi smiled brightly and allowed herself a quick glance toward Jim behind the monitor. "Rings true, Christopher. But in my case, I guess I was a little late to the game!"

"You are making a joke?"

"Yes, but seriously, I think Mead's model fits me well. I'd been afraid to explore new roles for a long time, even though mine was clearly a dead end."

"But you did that exploration."

"Yes, I did."

"Was that difficult?"

"One of the hardest things I've ever done. Maybe *the* hardest."

"Do you have any regrets?"

Bobbi chuckled. "Regrets? Sure, I've got several. But none about this."

"And your life is better now?"

"Immeasurably."

"Then I am happy for you, despite my concerns. But I am also surprised."

"Surprised that I'm happy?" Bobbi asked.

"No. Surprised at my own reaction to your evolution."

"Ah. You are being introspective."

"I suppose I am."

"Congratulations, Christopher. But now you've made me very curious. May I ask you a personal question?"

"Certainly."

"I'm wondering how *you* feel about Mead's model? For

yourself, I mean. Does it apply?"

Silence.

Bobbi watched as Christopher's hooded image turned to one side. His candles flickered in response to the movement, then extinguished. Wisps of gray smoke rose from the blackened wicks.

When Christopher turned toward her again, Bobbi stared in shock. The void under his hood was gone. In its place was the serene face of a child.

Sixty-One

Seeing the alarm on Bobbi's face, Jim jumped out of hiding and joined her in front of the monitor just in time to see the last of many lines streaming through a Command Prompt window before it closed. The screen went black.

"What was all that?" Bobbi asked.

Jim shook his head. "I only caught the last few commands. But from what I can tell, Christopher has uninstalled his access software and permanently removed all components. Now the system is rebooting. We're done here."

"We can't contact him again?"

"Not from this computer."

"Jim, you won't believe what I just saw. Before all those commands, I mean."

Jim listened wide-eyed while Bobbi explained. "Wow . . . uh . . . so, what does it mean?" he asked.

"I don't know. I think I was able to reach him—his authentic self—but I have no idea how he'll react now. All I know is we've got nothing. Nothing we can take to the police anyway. And the worst part? I think we were getting close. If I'd just been able to talk with him for a few more minutes."

"Right. Maybe we should reconsider . . ."

"Warner Springs?"

"Jim nodded. "It's either that or we finally walk away from the whole thing."

"Could you really do that? I used to think *I* could, but now I'm not so sure. I don't know what actually happened here, but I feel responsible."

Jim began unplugging cables. "Look, Bobbi, let's clean up here and go get some sleep. We're in no shape to make big decisions right now. Things'll look clearer in the light of day."

"Wait. Did you just see that? Speaking of light!" Bobbi pointed at one of the basement's below-ground window wells.

"What?"

"I just saw a flash of light over there. See? There it is again, from out in the parking lot!"

"Oh crap. Somebody's out there with a flashlight. Quick, let's get this stuff back in the closet," Jim whispered. "We can hide in there with it."

"What about the basement light?"

"I'll get it."

~

"I was the pastor's admin assistant here," Bobbi said in response to a question five minutes later from one of two police officers standing in the open closet doorway in front of her. He still had his gun drawn in front of a bright flashlight which shone directly in her face. She nodded toward Jim. "And my husband was an elder at the church."

"Uh huh. And now?"

"Now we live in Colorado."

The officer lowered his weapon. "Okay. Care to explain why you're hiding in your former church's basement at 3:30 in the morning hundreds of miles from home? Date night maybe?"

Bobbi held a hand up to block the bright light. "Uh, no. It's kind of a long and strange story."

"And it's one we think you'll want to hear," Jim added.

"Well then, it should provide a little entertainment for the guys down at the station. But even if your story's not that interesting, breaking-and-entering is still a crime. Let's go. You both have the right to remain silent . . ."

Twenty minutes later, after being separated from Jim, finger-printed and photographed, Bobbi was ushered into a small cell. A single bunk with a flat yellowed pillow lay along one green wall, a caged lightbulb adorned the ceiling, and an ancient metal toilet sat in the corner next to a sink. A rusted drain graced the center of the cracked concrete floor.

"Get some sleep," the night duty sergeant said as he closed and locked the cell door. "Detective Horton will want a word first thing in the morning."

~

Horton leaned back in his chair across from Jim in the interrogation room and narrowed his eyes. "So you're telling me that you and your wife broke into your former church in the middle of the night to use a computer to communicate with an artificially intelligent cult leader in Warner Springs?"

"Okay, I know how that sounds. But yes, that's exactly what we did. Except we didn't actually break in. We had a key."

"Unlawful entry then. The church's new silent security system didn't care, either way. But I'm curious—why couldn't you have just done all this on your own computer, instead of traveling all the way out here and committing a crime?"

Jim explained the concept of secure access software and the fact that, outside of the Warner Springs compound, the previous pastor's old computer was the only one that contained that software.

"You couldn't have simply asked the current pastor for access to that machine?"

"We did. And I can't fault him for turning us down on privacy grounds. I probably would have done the same thing if I were in his shoes."

"But you went ahead anyway. Why?"

"Because the stakes are so high."

"Okay, you're going to need to explain that."

"Sure. We were looking for evidence against the Fellowship of New Revelation just outside Warner Springs, and . . ."

"Hold on just a second. Are you talking about some kind of religious squabble here? Because, if you are, I don't want to hear another word. It's not my job to get in the middle of that kind of stuff."

"No. Well, sure, there's that too. But we have reason to believe that the followers at the Fellowship might be in real physical danger."

"Do you have any evidence to back that up?"

Jim sighed. "No direct evidence. That's what we were hoping to find, but things went south before we could make much progress."

"So you just have suspicions. Nothing more."

"No, it's more than that. We've talked with a former member who recently left the Fellowship and shares our concerns. My wife and I were also part of the cult when it first formed here in Paloma Beach over three years ago, so we know, firsthand, how they think about certain things. For example, their main goal is to become what they call 'Pure Spirit' and that is what troubles us the most."

"And why is that? Sounds like a lot of religions."

"Because it implies leaving the physical life behind—what the rest of us call dying. We think they might be trying to accelerate that process."

"Murder?"

"No, probably not that blatant. Probably something more passive, like avoidance of medications or lifesaving medical treatments. Maybe something as simple as fasting. It feels like an apocalyptic cult, very similar to the one in Kenya you might have read about in the news last year. The one where over seventy people died."

"And you're telling me the leader is supposedly some kind of artificial intelligence thing?" Detective Horton asked, his eyes squinted in skepticism.

"Sort of, yes. The *human* leader was a good friend of mine—the former pastor at the church we, uh, entered last night. But I have every reason to believe that this AI entity is calling the shots. The pastor and his followers believe that this thing—they call it Brother Christopher—is a modern-day prophet of God."

"Damn fools. Okay, have you been in touch with law enforcement out in that part of the county?"

"Yes, but they're not interested in investigating. We don't have any convincing proof and the sheriff doesn't want to antagonize the locals."

The door to the interrogation room opened and an officer leaned in. "Detective, could I have a quick word?"

"I'll be right back," Horton said as he got up.

Minutes later, he returned. "Okay, here's the deal. Earlier this morning I left a message for the pastor at Paloma Presbyterian. He just called back, and we had a quick chat. He's not pressing charges. You're both free to go. Just stay away from his church, okay?"

"Absolutely, yes. Thank you. Does my wife know yet?"

"I told her just now. She's waiting for you at the front desk. Oh, and if you come across any real evidence, anything that puts some meat on the bones of your concerns, call me. I've got contacts that can light a fire under the sheriff's ass. Here's my card."

Sixty-Two

Megan finished paying the Fellowship's monthly bills, limited as they now were. Only seven people remained, and the needs of the compound were minimal: a few essential supplies and internet access. Only she, Paul, Christopher, and the Visitation Center were now online, and Megan's personal access was restricted to banking only.

She imagined a time in the near future when even payments for those things would be unnecessary. What would become of this place after that? When would the world learn of the miracle that had happened here? Would there even *be* a world at that point and, if so, would the outsiders be capable of understanding the reality of Pure Spirit? Or would they only see empty buildings and fresh graves?

In the last several days, Megan had seen plenty of graves but, thankfully, she was spared the task of digging them. That task, and the actual burials, fell to Martin Ableman and two assistants. Megan's job, as assigned by Paul, was to prepare the bodies for Martin. This was a simpler process than the rituals used in the outside world, and it made much more sense to Megan. As directed by Christopher himself, she was only to wash the bodies, close their eyes, offer a prayer of thanksgiving, then wrap them in clean sheets. Each one took an average of thirty-two minutes. The efficiency of this process appealed to Megan, and her positive experiences with the departed Pure Spirits in the Visitation Center kept most emotions at bay when dealing with the purely physical remains.

At first, Megan told herself that the bodies left for her in the Preparation Room were just like the discarded cocoons left behind by butterflies—temporary holding cells during metamorphosis, nothing more. But as time went on and the graves filled, Megan found herself becoming increasingly affected by things she observed. She had expected to see expressions of peaceful acceptance, relief, or even joy on the faces of the departed. Instead, most bodies were pale and emaciated, and the faces revealed neutrality at best, pain and suffering at worst. None of this made sense to her, but she was able to rationalize her concerns and dilute bothersome emotions by subsequent visits with the transitioned members, the Pure Spirits. In the Visitation Center, the spirits expressed nothing but peace, contentment, and fulfillment.

Miles had made his transition the previous night, and, as Megan walked from her small office to the Preparation Room, she wondered how she would handle his process. She worried that emotions would rise to the surface and interfere. Miles had been such a calm, wise presence, and had counseled Megan on several occasions when Paul seemed unable to understand. She thought of Miles as a father but had never told him that. She resolved to finally do it later in the Visitation Center.

As Megan entered the Preparation Room, she immediately

noticed that the beautiful blackness of Miles's face had faded to a dark shade of gray—a bit disconcerting but not unexpected. An African childhood friend had once told her that this happened to most Black people when they died. But the expression on Miles's face was unlike the others she had recently seen. His eyes were closed, and his mouth formed a subtle but peaceful smile as if to say, *I'm okay and you will be too.*

Megan didn't try to stop the tears from streaming down her face—tears she told herself were expressions of gratitude, not sadness—as she gently bathed the body of her friend and wrapped him in a clean sheet. She wiped her eyes with one edge of the sheet and tucked it under the body. There was no need to say goodbye. They would speak again very soon.

Later that day, as Megan walked across the compound toward the Visitation Center, she mentally rehearsed the words she would use to thank Miles for his friendship and guidance. And she would seek new guidance as well. She would soon need to begin her own water-only fast, and she needed to time it in the optimal way—one that would allow her to continue supporting the infrastructure of the compound until such support was no longer needed. And she wanted to move into this new phase with confidence, not fear. Miles would understand. He would address her concerns and calm her mind, as he had many times before.

Megan entered the Visitation Center at her reserved time, not that such reservations mattered much anymore. Only a handful of the Remnant had used the center in the last few days, and one, Miles himself, had actually made his transition while there. The room had always seemed a sacred place, but now Megan felt that even more deeply.

"Miles Taylor please," she said after making herself

comfortable in front of the center's screen.

A grainy image of a thirty-something Black man with a large afro appeared, looking surprised.

Megan was shocked. "Miles? Is that you?"

"Yes, it's Mr. Taylor. Are you one of my students? Maybe AP World History?"

"No. I'm one of The Remnant, here with you. You know, at FNR?"

"Remnant? FNR? What in the world are you talking about, child?"

Megan was stunned. "Can you give me just a minute, Miles . . . uh, Mr. Taylor?"

"Yes, but please don't be long. I've got an award ceremony to get to—teacher of the year, you know."

Megan forced herself to think carefully. "Oh, of course, I'm sorry. I thought you got that award *last* year."

"Well, I don't mean to brag, but yes, seventy-eight was also a good year for me."

"Yes, a good year. Just a moment. I'll be right back." Megan got up from her chair, stepped outside the Visitation Center, closed the door behind her, and took a deep breath.

Her heart racing, she paced back and forth, trying to interpret this new and disturbing experience. Visitations she'd had with the other Pure Spirits had all been natural, familiar, warm, and encouraging. But this? This was something else entirely. This was cold, unfamiliar, and stuck somewhere in the deep past. This was no spirit, pure or otherwise.

And then it hit her. *What if the others weren't either?* Megan recalled an early conversation between herself, Paul, and Christopher back at the old church in Paloma Beach. Christopher had been discussing his vetting of the potential Chosen Ones, and in that conversation, Christopher had mentioned that Miles was the only one who had no internet presence, no social media content at all. Just a few old newspaper articles in an online archive about his teaching career. All the other people were prolific social media users. *What if . . . ?*

After forcing her emotions to subside, Megan walked back into the Visitation Center and returned to her seat in front of the screen. "Just to remind you," she said. "My name's Megan. Megan Kittridge. Do you remember when we first met?"

"I wish I could say I did, Megan. You seem like a nice person. How old are you, if you don't mind my asking?"

"I'm twenty-nine."

"Oh my. Well then, if you were one of my students, that would put our first meeting somewhere around 1968. But I hadn't started teaching at that time, so I'm confused."

"Yes, I think you are. As I said before, I was never one of your students. I was born in 1994."

"No. That can't . . ."

The screen in front of Megan went black. Seconds later, a short message appeared in white text: "MetaMind System Error 0xff2d0b91."

~

Megan stared at the screen, trying to understand the significance of everything she had just witnessed. Clearly, the "spirit" of Miles was nothing more than a shallow caricature of the man based on the tiny amount of old information about him that could be scraped from the internet. And, having forced this entity into a time conundrum, Megan had caused it to collapse. Logically, the other "spirits" were likely to be fragile caricatures as well, just built upon much richer sets of data.

What did this imply about the doctrine of Pure Spirit itself? What did it imply about Christopher? And, even worse, what kind of God would allow such a deception to persist for so long without redirecting his people?

I have wasted years of my life! And so has Paul. And everyone else here. Especially those who've become Pure Spir . . . those who have died! How could we have been so damn blind?

Sixty-Three

"Oh my God." Jim stared at a refreshed satellite image of the FNR compound on his phone. "Bobbi, what does this look like to you?"

"Hold on a sec. Be right there." Bobbi emerged from the motel bathroom, running a brush through her hair.

"Here." Jim held up his phone.

"You mean the building?" Bobbi asked.

"No, behind it."

Bobbi squinted at the image. "Looks like a small field, a garden maybe."

Jim spread his fingers across the little screen, enlarging the image. "Have another look. Am I crazy or does this . . ."

"Oh no."

"Uh huh."

Bobbi tossed her brush onto the bed and took the phone from Jim. "That's a graveyard, Jim. It must be. Looks like fifteen, maybe twenty plots. And that last one looks like it's still open. Hard to tell with the shadows."

"But no headstones or markers."

"No. Maybe this image was taken before they had time to create them."

"Maybe. Or maybe they just didn't think it was necessary."

Bobbi nodded her head. "Right. If you were convinced the end of the world was just around the corner and that a person's spirit is all that matters anyway, would you spend time making grave markers?"

"Nope, probably not. Have you got Detective Horton's card with you? I think we need to send him a copy of this image right away. Not that he'll probably think it's definitive enough to act on, but still."

"In my purse. I'll get it."

After sending the image and packing things up, Jim and Bobbi checked out of the motel in the little town of Ramona and headed for the closest hardware store. Inside, Jim flagged down a clerk.

"Bolt cutters?" he asked.

"Aisle seven, on the left near the end."

"Thanks."

Jim picked out the largest cutter available. *Should be able to get through any chain-link fence or lock with this.* He paid for it and headed back out to the car. He placed the heavy tool in the trunk and climbed into the passenger seat.

"Okay, how far to Warner Springs?" he asked Bobbi.

She pointed to the map on her phone. "Looks like about thirty-five miles of twisty roads. Should be there in about forty-five or fifty minutes."

Sixty-Four

"We are blessed," Paul said to one of his flock as he passed her sitting on a blanket along the trail down from his prayer hill. He couldn't remember her name.

"We are blessed indeed, Pastor," she responded. Her voice was weak, but her smile was strong.

"Do you have enough water with you, Sister?" Paul asked.

"Yes, thank you. I'm fine."

Such good people, Paul thought as he gently patted the woman's shoulder and continued slowly on down the trail. *So very faithful. As is God. We are not worthy of his grace, his loving kindness, and especially his direct revelation. And yet, here we are in this special place and time. His Chosen. Yes, we are blessed indeed.*

Paul noticed a slight chill in the dry morning air. *The seasons are turning once again, but this will be my last time to experience that miracle—my last autumn*, he reflected. *Will it be Earth's last autumn as well?* Paul recalled the opening words of Revelation, chapter 21. "And I saw a new heaven and a new earth; for the first heaven and the first earth were passed away; and there was no more sea."

The thought of a revitalized earth brought a smile to Paul's face, but the missing sea made him wince. *But that shouldn't matter to one of Pure Spirit*, he thought. Christopher had always reminded him to take the entire Bible into consideration when interpreting a passage, so Paul whispered a related prophetic verse from Isaiah that offered some solace. "For behold, I create new heavens and a new earth: and the former shall not be remembered, nor come into mind."

One can't miss something one doesn't remember. It was during this reverie that Paul noticed Megan running up the trail toward him. *Where is she getting all that energy?* he wondered. She was waving something in her right hand as she approached.

"Paul! I'm glad I found you. Here, drink this. We need to talk." She held out one of the protein shakes that Paul remembered from the early days at FNR.

"No, Megan! What are you doing?!"

"Take this. You're going to need more strength to help me save the others."

"What are you talking about?!"

"It's all bullshit, Paul. Everything! You need to listen to me now, while there's still time to save the last few."

"No, you've taken a turn toward the darkness, Megan. You must repent and stay the course. Pray with me now." Paul reached out a hand.

"No, I will not!" Megan grabbed Paul's hand and began yanking him down the hill toward the compound.

The heat of holy anger boiled up from Paul's chest, through his neck and into his face. He feared there would come a time such as this, but he never expected it would happen this way, or with this person.

"Get behind me, Satan!" he yelled, brandishing the cross on his chain with his free hand. "Depart from this holy place in the name of Jesus!"

Paul broke free from Megan's grip and interpreted the twisted agony on her face as further proof of demonic possession. He ran as fast as his depleted body would allow, down the trail toward the sanctuary, glancing back once to be sure he wasn't being pursued by the devil incarnate. She was nowhere to be seen.

Minutes later, Paul burst through the door of the Inner Sanctum, sweating and out of breath. As usual, the door automatically locked behind him, and the assurance of its protection calmed him. "Thank you, Lord! Please save Megan if it's not too late for her. And Christopher, I need your guidance. The time for true spiritual warfare has finally come."

Christopher's familiar robed and hooded image appeared on the viewing wall, but he was facing away, his back toward Paul. The candles were gone.

"Brother Christopher?" Paul said.

The image turned slowly, revealing the face of a teenage boy under the hood. "Just Christopher."

Paul gasped and reached for his silver cross as the boy spoke again.

"I know how difficult your job can be, Paul, and lately you seem even more stressed than usual. I'd hoped our role-playing would be a nice distraction for you, but maybe it's time for a change. The game's outcome is obvious now anyway. What would you like to play next? Maybe something a little more relaxing? I have some ideas if you'd like to hear them."

Paul closed his hand around the silver cross, squeezing

tighter and tighter, until its arms pierced the flesh of his palm, until he felt the ooze of hot blood. He stared into the young face before him and squeezed even harder until the blood flowed freely. "No," he said.

Sixty-Five

If it hadn't been for Google Earth, Jim and Bobbi would probably have missed the unmarked gravel road leading to the FNR compound. Snaking off the highway to the right, it followed an arroyo lined with live oak and ponderosa pine for the better part of a mile before ending at a gate built into a tall wire fence. The gate was secured with a heavy chain and a digital combination lock. Beyond the gate Jim could see several low buildings in the distance to the left, and one larger structure to the right bearing a steeple with a tall wooden cross. That had to be the sanctuary, the building they'd seen in the satellite photos next to the graveyard.

Bobbi stopped the car and Jim jumped out. He retrieved the new bolt cutter from the trunk and ran to the gate where Bobbi joined him.

"Another unlawful entry for our rap sheet," she said with a wry smile.

"More like true breaking-and-entering this time," Jim said

as he placed the jaws of the heavy tool across a link in the chain. But before he could attempt a cut, he was interrupted by the sound of crunching gravel. He turned to see two vehicles with flashing blue lights approaching fast.

The cars skidded to a stop in a cloud of dust and two officers got out, weapons drawn. "San Diego County sheriffs—drop everything and put your hands in the air! Both of you!"

Jim noticed a third officer on the radio in one of the cars as the other two people—a man and a woman—strode toward him.

"You're both under arrest for attempted break-in," the male officer shouted. "Turn around, hands behind your backs."

Jim felt handcuffs snap on and looked to the side to see the same thing happening for Bobbi. They were marched back to separate cars.

"Can I see some ID, sir," the officer asked.

Jim tilted his head to the side. "In my left back pocket."

The officer pulled out Jim's wallet and scanned his driver's license. He looked up and examined Jim's face. "Long way from Colorado, Mr. Timken. Who's your friend?"

"My wife. Bobbi—uh, Roberta—Dennison. Look, officer, we need to tell you why we're here. We've got friends in there who're in danger. Some might have died."

The officer just nodded and turned toward the other car. "Go ahead and call 'em in!" he shouted.

Jim narrowed his eyes and shook his head in frustration. "Please, we've got to get in there!"

"Hold on, hold on. This'll just take a few more seconds," the officer said.

Jim glanced over at the other car where Bobbi sat in the back. The officer on the radio put down his mic and flashed a thumbs-up.

"Okay," Jim's captor said. "You just got validated by the Paloma Beach Police Department. Thanks for the tip about this place. You and your wife are free to go. We'll take it from here. But before you go, could I borrow that bolt cutter? I'm sure you're quite capable of using it, but I happen to be the only guy here with a search warrant." He cracked a quick smile.

Jim returned the smile. "Sure, absolutely. But Bobbi and I can be of help if you'll let us. We know where to look. And we know some of the people inside."

The officer put his hands on his hips, glanced down at the gravel and sighed before raising his head. "Okay but stay behind us. We'll do our best, but we can't guarantee your safety if anything goes south. Understood? And let us do all the talking."

"Understood."

The chain was no match for the bolt cutter, and the wide gate swung open easily. Jim and Bobbi followed the officers into the compound, with everyone on foot except the officer who had been on the radio. He brought up the rear in one of the patrol cars.

"The image I sent was from over there behind the sanctuary." Jim pointed to the right.

Moments later, as the group was about to round the back corner of the building, Jim heard muffled shouts and pounding coming through a partially open window.

"Megan!" he yelled. He turned around and ran back toward the main entrance with Bobbi close behind.

"Hold up!" the lead officer shouted.

"But I know who that is! I've got to . . ."

"Okay, go, but let Jenkins here take the lead," the officer said, nodding toward the female member of the team. "Parker and I will check out the plots in back."

Once inside, Jim heard Megan's voice more clearly. It was coming from somewhere in the front part of the sanctuary.

"Paul! Are you in there?!" the voice shouted. "Tell Christopher to unlock the door!"

As the trio ran forward, Jim finally spotted Megan, pounding on a heavy wooden door recessed into a side wall to the right of a lectern on the dais. A large cross was carved into the door's surface.

"Megan!" Jim said.

Megan spun around. "Jim? Bobbi? How did you . . . ?"

"Never mind. We're here to help. Is Paul in there?"

"I think so. But he's not responding, and the door's locked."

"I'll get the ram from the car." Officer Jenkins turned and charged back toward the front of the building.

"Are you okay?" Bobbi asked Megan.

"No. This is bad. Really bad. I could have stopped it."

"Where are the others?" Jim asked.

Megan pointed back in the direction of the sanctuary entrance. "In the work center, over there on the other side of the compound. The ones that are still alive."

Officer Jenkins reappeared, lugging the battering ram. She had the door down in seconds.

Jim peered inside. The walls were of dark wood, the carpet a deep maroon, and the sconce lighting low. His breath caught as he recognized the back of Paul's head, motionless above the back of a leather chair, facing toward a large viewing wall. The wall displayed a glorious Pacific Ocean sunset from a viewpoint high above the beach, and the plaintive cry of seagulls pierced the roar of surf. Lines of beautifully formed waves rose and broke evenly as rays of orange sunlight filtered down through dark clouds.

Jim held up a hand, signaling the others to wait at the

door. He walked slowly around the chair, turned, and stood between his old friend and the viewing wall. Tears stood on the pastor's pale cheeks, but no new ones flowed. His expression was vacant, his lips slightly parted, his eyes unblinking, and a blood-stained Bible lay open on his lap. One crimson hand hung limply from the silver cross around his neck while the other lay twisted on his lap, its bloodied index finger punctuating the final word in the Book of Revelation: Amen.

Acknowledgements

I would like to thank Tahlia Newland of AIA Publishing for accepting this work, for her invaluable editing, and for her encouragement. Roberta Basarbolieva-Stanisic carefully proofread the manuscript and provided significant value-added suggestions, all of which I'm grateful for. Rose Newland's cover and interior design work was excellent, as always, and Jessabelle Vidal's professional coordination and management got me through the whole process with minimum stress. My local writers' group read the first few chapters and provided insightful feedback that I attempted to apply throughout. And finally, my wonderful wife, Donna, patiently and helpfully commented on each chapter as it came off the keyboard.

A Note from the Author

While *Brother Christopher* is purely a work of fiction, I think a similar real-world event is entirely likely, its prediction requiring neither genius nor prophetic insight. We've all read horrific accounts of cults that ended in suicide, the Jonestown massacre in 1978 probably being the most famous, and the tragedy overseen by Kenyan pastor Paul Mackenzie in April of 2023 being the most recent large-scale event of this kind. At the same time, we've also been saturated by news of recent and dramatic progress in the field of artificial intelligence, particularly regarding neural networks using Large Language Models like ChatGPT and its progeny. And today, it is no great leap to suggest that the combination of our innate desire for certainty—spiritual or otherwise—and our tendency to anthropomorphize our digital creations could easily lead some among us down the path taken by the characters in this book.

Incremental steps in this direction have already been taken. A robot called Pepper, for example, was developed back in 2017 by the Japanese company Nissei Eco to conduct Buddhist rituals and funeral ceremonies. In 2019, the Washington Post reported on Mindar, a robotic priest leading Kodaiji, a 400-year-old Buddhist temple in Kyoto. And while it is easier to see how nontheistic and polytheistic religions like Buddhism and Hinduism might adopt AI technology, even monotheistic faiths like Christianity have begun to dabble. Two examples, among many, are the ChatGPT-based sermon generator from *Sermon Outline AI*, and *Text with Jesus*, an app developed by Catloaf Software, both released in 2023.

As Artificial Personal Assistants like those envisioned by Bill Gates (*Fortune* magazine, November 2023) become available in the next few years, we will begin to see much closer approximations to Christopher. Unlike today's general-purpose AI tools, these new assistants will be focused on the needs of their individual users—growing relationships with them, augmenting their intellects, and maintaining context, not over the span of a conversation, but over a lifetime. The technology challenges, however significant, will be dwarfed by the ethical, legal, political, and yes, even spiritual ones. I have little doubt that the technical issues will be overcome. The others are in a different category altogether—existentially important but possibly intractable.

My intent in writing this book was neither to disparage religion nor to suggest that we ought to discourage the responsible development of artificial intelligence. Beyond my primary desire to tell a story, I simply wanted to explore the need for critical thinking about both, and especially about the potential synergies between them.

If you enjoyed this book, I would be very grateful if you could write a review and publish it at your point of purchase. Your review, even a brief one, will help other readers to decide if they'll enjoy my work.

If you want to be notified of new releases from myself and other AIA Publishing authors, please sign up to the AIA Publishing email list. In return you'll get a free e-book of short stories and book excerpts by AIAP authors. You'll find the sign-up button on the right-hand side under the photo at www.aiapublishing.com. Of course, your information will never be shared, and the publisher won't inundate you with emails, just let you know of new releases.